Praise for Jim Powell and *Only Witness*

Jim Powell's book of stories, *Only Witness*, bears insightful and lyrical witness to the everyday comedy and tragedy of our time, with an admirably authentic Hoosier flavor. Powell joins the great tradition of Nicholson, Tarkington and Vonnegut.

—Dan Wakefield, author of *Going All the Way*

The stories in *Only Witness* reveal Jim Powell's finely-honed observational skills. He witnesses children, young people on the prowl, families, a woman married to a sex addict, the son of a woman with Alzheimer's, and more. I am charmed and moved by these stories. Some are tender-hearted and funny, some keenly honest and tough-minded. Buy this book and prepare to be entertained!

—Patricia Henley, author of *In the River Sweet* and
Other Heartbreaks

An impressive collection of short stories and vignettes, *Only Witness* takes the reader from the United States and Mexico to Eastern Europe and beyond. Some stories embrace straight-up realism, exploring life in euchre-playing small-town Midwest, while others go so far as to be told through the perspective of a jealous snake charmer's cobra in a traveling reptile zoo. Jim Powell makes a fine debut in this wide-ranging collection of short fiction.

—Tony Ardizzone, author of *The Whale Chaser*

The witnesses in this book testify to the innocence of human nature, and how it is too often betrayed. These stories ring with compassion and empathy. The characters are tightly drawn and their surroundings painted in psychological color. Powell ponders that conflict most common to us all, the tug of war between desire and responsibility, lust and legitimacy. For the reader there is satisfaction in knowing that these moral dilemmas have been carefully studied, weighed and balanced, witnessed if not resolved. Intimacy prevails, and in the end one gets a sense of guarded peace, that everything is operating normally in the world, or at least well enough to get us by. We want to applaud the writer for stories that resonate.

—James Thomas, coeditor of the *Sudden Fiction* and *Flash Fiction* anthology series.

Jim Powell has long served Indiana literature—both in his support of emerging writers and his knowledge and insight into the historical canon, which he has helped define. And now in this new collection of short fiction, he adds his own unique voice to the list of writers who bear witness to this particular place. Even when his characters leave the Midwest for Europe, Mexico, or California, in remarkable Chekhovian stories such as "Night Train to Vienna," "Klezmer Music" and "The Cardsellers," their Midwestern sensibilities travel with them, transforming and interrogating all they see.

—Susan Neville, author of *Sailing the Inland Sea*

Hear me out on this: I believe Jim Powell demonstrates with the urbane fictions collected in *Only Witness* that we are in the presence of a contemporary Henry James. Listen: time after time, Powell's stories perform these exquisite Jamesian pas de deux of perceptions and amplifications. The slightest of slights, the gist of pure gesture found in these fictions explicate the unsettled sighs of Expats and the polite ululations of our alienated neighbors behind their next doors. They all stoically search through the fractured aesthetics and distressed detritus of late capitalism and the dying Holocene. With sentences that are patient, profound, and precise, these stories of elegant understatement sustain us and have, against all odds, ramshackled staying power.

—Michael Martone, author of *Brooding* and
The Moon Over Wapakoneta

ONLY WITNESS

....

Stories by

Jim Powell

INwords Publications
Indianapolis · 2019

Copyright © 2019 by INWords Publications, Indiana Writers Center
All rights reserved.

ONLY WITNESS by Jim Powell
ISBN: 978-0-9967438-9-1

Edited by Barbara Shoup
Author photo by Natasha Hastings-Heinz
Cover photo by Benjamin Davies
Book design by Andrea Boucher

Printed in the United States of America

INwords PUBLICATIONS
PRESENTED BY THE INDIANA WRITERS CENTER

For Karen

ACKNOWLEDGMENTS

- "Toyland" first appeared in *Bartleby Snopes*, 2015.

- "Scouts" first appeared in *Crack the Spine*, 2017.

- "Little Roy's Roving Reptile Zoo" first appeared in *Fiction Southeast*, 2018.

- "Pyramid Scheme" first appeared in *Flying Island*, 2017.

- "Little Jungle" first appeared in *From the Edge of the Prairie*, 2017.

- "Tigerville" first appeared in *Storyscape*, 2017.

- "Desiree" first appeared in *Typehouse Literary Magazine*, 2019.

- "The Cardsellers" first appeared in *Windless Orchard*, 1983.

Grateful thanks to the Indiana Writers Center for this wonderful opportunity. The Writers Center centered my life for the twenty years of my directorship and it is especially gratifying to see how far the organization has come and how its programs have evolved beyond our original vision.

Special thanks to IWC director/publisher Barbara Shoup who has been essential to my growth as a writer through her perceptive criticism, editing, and encouragement.

I am grateful to the Arts Council of Indianapolis for a Creative Renewal Fellowship that allowed travel, which inspired several of the stories in this collection.

Thanks to my creative writing teachers: Arturo Vivante, Philip F. O'Conner, Robert Early, and John Clellon Holmes. Thanks as well to the hundreds of students who taught me as much about writing as I taught them.

For advice and encouragement, I thank my longtime friends and Bowling Green State compadres Leonard Durso, Randy Michael Signor, Tony Ardizzone, and James Thomas, and Indianapolis friends Dan Carpenter and Dan Wakefield.

For reading many drafts, her excellent editing and proofreading, not to mention the sustaining pies and the love, my eternal thanks to my wife Karen Kovacik.

INTRODUCTION

Jim Powell headed for California when he finished his MFA, assuming he had to move away from Indiana to be a real writer. Then, lucky us, he came home—where he fell into the role of literary leadership because he longed for a community of like minds, a place where writers could hone their craft. In1979 he founded the Free University Writers Center, which became the Writers Center of Indianapolis, incorporated in 1984—which morphed into the Indiana Writers Center.

During his twenty years as the Center's director, Jim Powell touched the lives of hundreds of Hoosier writers, including my own. His tireless efforts at promoting Indiana writers and their work were instrumental in establishing the lively and diverse literary scene we enjoy today.

But such dedication came at a cost: he stopped writing fiction. Following his involvement with the Writers Center, Powell taught composition and creative writing at IUPUI. Talking to his students about fiction—and a health scare in 2010—inspired him to return to his craft. Over the last nine years, he has written seventy stories. *Only Witness* is a collection of the very best of them.

Powell is an Indiana writer in the best sense. The stories in *Only Witness* range from a porch in Indianapolis to Vienna, Krakow, Puerto Vallarta, and beyond—but no matter its setting, each story is filtered through the lens of a writer who knows who he is and where he's from. Powell's stories are intense, even disturbing at times. But they are always true. Each one reflects the wisdom and generosity of a life lived, a witness to the vast complexity of the human condition.

For the past ten years, it has been an honor for me to serve as the executive director of the Indiana Writers Center, where Jim's legacy is alive and thriving. Given his lifelong support of Indiana writers, it seems fitting for the IWC to publish his first collection of stories as part of the celebration of our fortieth anniversary.

Reader, enjoy!

Barbara Shoup
Executive Director, Indiana Writers Center

CONTENTS

TIGERVILLE

THE ONE DAY OF THE WEEK YOU don't set the alarm you wake early anyway, hearing her in the kitchen stirring sugar and milk into her coffee. You pull on your hang-around-the-house clothes, making sure none of the cats have crept underfoot. You've called your house Tigerville since Cleo (the young feral you and she saved from February's ice storm) bit and drew blood, and your arm swelled to three times normal, sending you to emergency. Since then things seem to happen outside your will—catch-as-catch-can, come-as-you-are. It isn't the cats' fault, or hers. Only new animals, another human presence, your house a community now. For the first time one you do not rule.

You trudge downstairs carefully, fearing a fatal fall. The stairs seem steeper, the tread slipperier than before she moved in for a new year's beginning together. All she asked for was her own room where she could meditate and write.

She's already opened the living room drapes to April's bud-ding trees and the grass's vague greening. You inhale the coffee she's brewed then sniff the oily smell of her ritual lamp behind the closed door of her workspace, once an unused guest room. You catch a hint of her last night's bath, the sweet scent you now sleep with. But she meditates in the mornings, so you quietly pour a cup—the sugar bowl now always full!—and scan the boring headlines of the newspaper she's brought in. The silence here in Tigerville makes you wonder what she's thinking.

You look around for the three cats, but only puffs of fur betray them. She's let them outside into the warm morning to reclaim their wild domain. You sip the coffee, look toward the alley where a redbud and yellow forsythia brighten the garage. Nature blooms without worrying over frost. You step onto the deck, listen for traffic's hum then remember that Saturday's near silence should offer comfort, not concern. She's hung baskets of flowers around the house, only yesterday placed pots of herbs that flavor the air. You breathe in the complicated aroma. Surrounded by so much beauty, why this unease? You scan the sky for weather, dramatic storm preferred, but find only white wisps of clouds. The day might drive you crazy with its calm. You sip the pungent coffee, stronger than you used to make for yourself.

Two squirrels playing tag leap from the neighbor's old maple to attack the garage roof with chirps and claws. From some distance a bird twitters, though the hawks of last summer—not seen this year—perhaps still warn intruders off. You were once a hawk yourself, hungry and intent, the authentic self you often preach to her.

One of her cats, Desdemona, creeps over the roof's ridge, black body sinuous. The squirrels scamper into the redbud's spindly branches. Surely Ophelia will appear next. Young Cleopatra must be lounging near the puddles in the neighbor's yard. Her older cats' predatory personalities showed to him clearly within a week of their arrival with her. Then Cleo's bite demonstrated *her* sense of play. Their suspicion of you—the masculine—is no surprise, but today in warmer weather the squirrels prove more engaging prey. The cats ignore you.

You sip and watch her puzzling over words at her desk, leaning back in the chair she chose for its uncomfortable uprightness. You wonder at her focus, her distance. She is near, but her self-absorption equals power. You don't want to interrupt—even to speak softly would seem a complaint. And you aren't really complaining, are you? You finish the strong sweet coffee and listen for movement in the house, but no sound relieves your isolation.

Ophelia pads from the maple onto the garage roof and Mona, creeping, glances back, nodding in conspiracy. The two squirrels in the redbud chatter. No cat can catch a squirrel unless it lets her. The cats sneak closer, spacing themselves, Ophelia down near the gutter, Mona slithering up, so they cover the squirrels' branch on both sides, though not upward. Squirrels have the sense to avoid traps. You stand, cornered by their drama. You shake your head, wishing the cats could somehow win.

But Ophelia leaps and Mona pounces into the tree, and the squirrels skitter higher then jump back onto the roof's ridge then into the maple. The cats pursue, but stop short at the roof's edge. They pose as if victorious—territory defended?—as the squirrels rattle branches in a vine-covered oak a backyard farther down the alley.

The cats puff their chests, descend via the redbud onto the ground then amble up the stairs onto the deck. The screen door clatters and the air moves as she comes up behind you.

"What's going on?" she asks. "Exciting kitty action here in Tigerville?" She kneels and the two older cats trot to her. She looks up and smiles, and you find yourself nodding like a fool.

"Squirrels gone wild." You point toward the trees. "Life in the jungle." You bend beside her and pet the cats. Cleopatra jumps onto the deck, lands with a thud by a pot of catnip then marches to the group. You reach out and she slips under your hand, fur still winter-thick. Ophelia and Desdemona meow greetings. They've taken to the little wild one like elder sisters.

She stands and you follow, inhaling the warmth she gives off. She nods at your coffee and takes the empty cup from your hand. She sets it on the glass table messy with pollen and seed pods. She puts her arms around you and you feel a moment of lust at her softness. The cats rub against your ankles, mewing, ready to be fed. This is what she's made you. Whatever this is.

LITTLE ROY'S ROVING REPTILE ZOO

L ITTLE ROY IS NOT SO LITTLE, NEVER slim like us serpents, and bigger in the britches since the Reptile Zoo pulled up stakes from LaFargeville near the 1000 Islands and added "Roving" to our name. May be he's not paying attention as his eighteen-year-old, sweet Roy Junior, is growing, too—growing up too fast as our travel stretches his horizons. This weekend, we're camped out in the greensward beside Buck's Eat Here and Get Gas in Wooster, Ohio. One night open and already the Zoo's garnered fans, in particular one who seems a bit too interested, name of Evie.

I have my interests, too. My name's Maya, the favorite cobra on the snake-charmer's team—Little Roy's storytellin' wife Scheherazade—so I spend time in a comfy woven basket as well as my glass display. I see and sense things, the human dynamic much more entertaining than our own slithers and hissing. Oh, the Flying Dragon Brothers, draco lizards, across the aisle create a flutter now and then, and the ancient tortoise Granny offers sage advice on those rare occasions she lumbers by. Otherwise, we go about our reptilian business, the least showy show creatures you'll ever meet, if you'd wander across our stage's simulation of a lush jungle.

Human nature, our humans' and the customers', is the real show here. Just yesterday, this Evie showed up and, after she'd paid her $10 admission and toured our tents, talked Little Roy into having Junior give her a backstage tour. She tells him she's been interested in snakes since her childhood gerbil got eaten by her older brother's rosy boa. Her parents claimed it was a mistake but Evie then defended her turf with a ball python that had now outgrown her small bedroom and her parents' patience. She seemed taken with Junior, a few years younger and naïve regarding womankind, potential sweeties put off by his wingmen, us reptiles.

Then I caught Evie trying to kiss him beside the alligator snapping turtle's huge tank. A cobra has only one way to offer warning and I flared my hood and struck the glass but Junior had been charmed. He practically knocked over the small turtles' terrarium when Evie pressed her body against him. I prayed that Scheherazade or Little Roy would interrupt to save him, but Junior took off, as shaky on his feet as a bearded dragon in need of calcium. Evie caught her breath and stood beaming. Oh, people were supposedly tempted into such "sin" by one of my forebears, but this girl didn't need any help. She even winked at me.

Junior's the boy I've watched grow, and I'm just waiting for my chance to rise and straighten Evie out. Today she's back and Scheherazade isn't complaining. An extra pair of hands never hurt. The girl's cleaning out cages and exercising the tamest snakes. Really, there's little danger here, since all of us have been devenomed and Evie is hardly squeamish. She checks out Junior constantly, and the covert looks he returns warn me he's a goner.

But maybe Little Roy and Ms S actually want to pair Junior Roy up, to keep him happy so he doesn't go missing some upcoming morn in Indiana, Kentucky, or Tennessee. It's bad enough he's been home-schooled by folks with no real home. Math is keeping the ledger, language arts reading the Herpetologist's Guide, science lab the mix of diets. And the psychology practicum is tricking us to work for little more than warm lamps and weekly rats.

Would we be better off in the wild? I'm no philosopher but I think not. Most of us arrived in the Zoo from far worse captivities. Little Roy brags on taking in ophidian orphans abandoned when they outgrew a cage or frightened the new bride of an owner. I can attest that Scheherazade and I care for each other. She strokes my head, lets me wind around her strong arms, coos to me with warm breath. All of us nurtured in our fake wilderness. Even the mischievous tree monitor is given space to play, shown the forbearance parents grant their own children.

In fact, Little Roy is more apt to stare down a frisky customer than one of us. Last evening a boy of twelve made faces against my glass but Roy's bark chased him away. I tried to give Roy a smile, but how would he know what mine looks like? He's the boss man, but in a laissez-faire way, eyes open, pacing past our displays, pondering who knows what? To us, he's gentle, and everyone tries to stay on best behavior to thank him for our sustenance. Least I can do is look out for his kid.

But here is Evie again, smiling at me. "You're the special one, aren't you, cobra? Always dancing and twirling." She spins around a bit clumsily. "Music lover. Like me." I'm no critic, but it is cute. If she weren't tempting Junior I might even like her, as I'm fascinated by movement. I rise a bit and she steps back, her coordination askew.

"You okay?" Junior's voice calls from the doorway flap. Then he's right here, too, all attention on her.

"Just chatting up the cobra." She bends at the knee, a kind of curtsey. "I'm not sure he likes me."

"Oh, Maya's a she," Junior says, patting my glass.

Evie tilts her head and rolls her tongue, mimicking me. "I'd much rather talk to you, Junior Roy."

The kid smiles, soul lost to this sex thing. Some nights, when the work's all done, I see Little Roy and Madame S make eyes at each other. Then I'll hear (of course, cobras can't really hear, but we feel a universe of vibrations) their RV bouncing a ritual beat, followed by a morning of whistled tunes, chirps for the lizards, smiles all around. I wonder at the humanity of it, our serpentine conjugality as complex, our joining a savage rapture that may last for hours.

Anyway, there's still plenty of cleaning and feeding to do and Junior's a good son who gets right back to work, though his eyes keep meeting Evie's and their movements from tank to tank become a clumsy dance, theirs alone.

Tonight's show goes well. I am again beguiled by Scheherazade's pungi music, her own sinuous movements as she tempts me with the flute into the dramatic contortions that never fail to sway the audience. The Dragon Brothers glide between their makeshift trapezes. The alligator turtle chomps an easily trapped fish as he paddles across the kiddie-pool "lagoon." The tree monitor takes advantage of his temporary freedom to climb the potted redbud on loan from a local nursery. The geckos chase their crickets. The iguanas slither through tubes and leap low walls. And of course Little Roy displays his mastery, limbs enwrapped by a dozen slithering boas.

Now Junior Roy comes on stage with his giant python, to my surprise joined by Evie as his assistant, costumed as a Middle Eastern princess like Ms S. Little Roy's voice booms with pride as he announces Evie's addition to the Zoo. She'll be working with his talented son. Like a magician's helper, she curtseys and I recoil, wanting to sound alarms. Junior "wrestles" the big constrictor but soon flails on the sod in pretend panic. Evie rolls eyes wide and beckons the audience to whisper worried "ohs." Then she touches Junior's shoulder and he calms, regains control. The python slinks away and balls around itself, the displeasure in its hiss audible before Evie leads the crowd into applause.

Junior stands tall, stomps the ground to stake his victory claim. His eyes fly over the fans, his parents, our display tanks, then alight on Evie, who swells in her tight costume and gives a hippy shake not unlike my own sinuous moves. I wriggle to catch his eye, warn him that humans can be enraptured by one another as we serpents have been, our natural freedoms lost in exchange for creature comforts.

They grasp each other's hand and take a bow—together. He is lost and there's nothing I can do. Even if Evie eventually trains to become my charmer, my use of fangs would only provoke Junior Roy's protection. He was certain to fall someday and Evie seems sincere in her love of us serpents, perhaps also of him.

So I sidle against the glass, coil to make my colors shine, tap with my snout for their attention. I stretch out my tongue to tease the air and welcome Evie to our Zoo, bid her to share my secret knowledge: it's not always the charmer who leads the charmed.

NIGHT TRAIN TO VIENNA

KELLY LAY IN THE UPPER BUNK AND touched the sticky mess Adam had left on her inner thigh. Through the train's jostling, they'd sprawled in and out of his narrow lower bunk, no rhythm found until his climax. Then, when the train braked, their unbalanced suitcases smacked against the berth. Adam chuckled as he stood, pushed the cases back, and looked down on her, grinning. Did he want a compliment on his performance in such difficult circumstances? Instead he asked her if, since he was standing, didn't she want to climb up into her own bunk? He was soon fast asleep and she wide awake.

In the glow of the reading light, she wanted to have more … rapport. The train sex was his idea, proposed with a lame joke about joining the "mile-*wide*" club. Still, the act had silenced him, so no more of the prattle she'd endured for days about Eastern European "growth markets" post-communism. It was she who'd proposed the trip which began in her great-grandparents' Slavic homeland. She'd been amazed at the changes—bright cars and shiny skyscrapers—since her one teenage visit to a gray and sullen Warsaw. Why couldn't Adam just enjoy her wish to better know herself?

Now they were approaching the Czech-Austrian border, once again a hard-stop crossing because of some World Economic Forum meeting in Adam's choice of city, prosperous—and Western—Vienna. They would be asked only to open their compartment for the passport check, but Kelly hoped the tiny space didn't reek of sex. She touched the stickiness again and decided the bathroom was a must. Adam snorted and it was all she could do to not exhale "men." She wasn't as much tired of their half-dozen-years marriage as weighted with the realization that even people you love change in ways you can't control. Personal growth, they call it. Pairs' problems, she thought.

She climbed down the ladder, pulled on her robe and grabbed her makeup, then turned the doorlock. Air from the corridor blasted in, noisy and less than fresh. Humid June warmth lingered despite the breeze from the pathway's open window. Wheels on rails hummed, the rough ride in Poland upgraded only when they'd crossed into the Czech Republic.

She closed the door behind her, finding her balance within a few small steps. From the car's nearest end a tall man appeared, moving from the shadows toward her. The sliding picture windows beside her showed only the dark countryside of Moravia, rolling hills and farmland. There was nowhere to go, so she pressed her back against the windows as the man neared.

She surely looked a messy hell, but the stranger's dark face opened in a smile and his black eyes darted. "Peace be upon you," he said. He wore a short-sleeved shirt and jeans, his skin a dark deeper than any tan. Tunisia? Egypt? Libya? All countries in turmoil—positive kinds, everyone hoped. Kelly felt sympathy toward him, and smiled as he turned to pass her without touching. His body moved the air around her, his smell provocative like incense. *"Assalamu alaikum."* His voice seemed dreamy, as if remembering a native tongue.

She replied, *"Salaam,"* hoping her pronunciation was Arabic and not Hebrew. She felt girlish and hopelessly American as the man moved away down the corridor. She and Adam argued about language use while traveling. He said English was ubiquitous, pronouncing that word in syllables as if she didn't know it. She'd tried to learn at least basic greetings in Polish, German, and Italian for their trip, but most of the time she hadn't gotten out more than "hello" before the native speaker turned to English. Adam smiled at that, 'I told you so.' But the tall North African's smile praised her for trying. Then he walked on more quickly and disappeared through the door to the next car. She shook her head—where was his compartment?

At the end of the corridor the small metallic bathroom was unoccupied, thank God, though still tinged with the man's cologne. The little mirror in the bathroom offered a wavery image of her—hair mussed and skin red-blotched on her neck. One thin white line marked her right cheek like a scar—from pressing a scrunched pillow?

Adam no longer seemed to pay attention to what she looked like unless they were going out in public. He'd become quite insistent about her duty to look good in supporting him. She tried to iron out the mark but only reddened her face. Why did she care to look acceptable for a border crossing anyway? The African, an Egyptian rebel she fantasized, had found her attractive, hadn't he?

She wetted her hair and brushed it flat. She washed until her skin smoothed, then applied a touch of powder to her cheek. She tilted her head like a playful schoolgirl and glowed at the improvement.

Kelly pulled down her panties and ran warm water onto a paper towel to wash away Adam's goo. She raised the seat lid on the metallic toilet. On the blue plastic seat a spot of white glistened. She closed her eyes tight then dared look again. "Jesus," she said out loud, stomping once on the metallic floor to build courage. She wiped the glob of semen away and tossed the towel into the bowl, used another with soap to scrub the seat, then activated the flush.

She let out a deep breath, sat, and giggled. No wonder the man had looked so contented. Kelly felt the gentle rocking of the train and found herself imagining his swarthy hands at work as she cleaned herself, then touched more gently, thighs tightening and feet raised on toes. She bent forward and rocked with the swoosh of the wheels, her breathing speeding until she brought herself to orgasm. "Oh, Christ," she whispered. "Oh, fuck."

Kelly washed again and touched up her still reddened face. She brushed her teeth, adjusted her robe, and gave a last look at the toilet seat before closing the lid. In the corridor the sounds were louder and the swaying motion again ran up her legs. There was no dark man at the other end and she found their compartment midway, double-checked the number and pulled open the door as quietly as she could.

Adam still snored in the lower berth. The sex must have been really good for him. But her satisfaction—with herself or their relationship—seemed less clear. She climbed the ladder, imagining missing a step so her foot unsettled his prideful smile. They had become so … static, their boundaries like the two bunks, in the same room but unaligned. His franchise brokering business had begun with a free-trade coffee operation and added products from green cleaning supplies to free-range eggs. She was proud of him, even if he'd referred to their vacation as "market research." She kept at her job doing PR for local nonprofits—Adam approved of her useful expertise—and her ever-improving baking. They read intelligent books and discussed the world, if not so often as before. They had mutual friends. They had their parents. Good health. They traveled and seemed to grow and agreed they would wait to have children, though that would soon need reconsideration. Why were they waiting? If she got pregnant, maybe she could start one of those cupcake operations, become a most-of-the-time mom? She saw a checkoff list of the reasons she should be hopeful about her future. Composed by whom—her mother? Her priest? Oprah? She thought of the dark man in the hallway. Maybe she'd become a traveler, a linguist, a scandal? Adventurer—that had a nice ring to it!

Kelly threw herself into the bunk and huddled on the thin mattress beneath the thin blanket. Her knees extended over the edge as she curled up, sniffing the air for their scent. She wished there were springs to turn into creaks and moans to haunt Adam's dreaming. But the rails hummed and she drifted into a shallow sleep.

The train clattered to a stop that again sent their suitcases crashing against the berth. Adam said, "Crap," and grumbled. He was not a morning person, even nearing his idyllic Vienna, Kelly observed with glee. She stretched toward the dawn glinting under the window shade. But when Adam pulled the shade up, and she descended and scanned the scene, it showed the artificial light of a station—Breclav/Hohenau, a sign read. The border crossing.

Adam put his hands on her ass and squeezed, making her jump against the flimsy shade. "Don't." She reached around him, pulled her robe from the hook, and tied it tight.

"Looks like we're almost back into civilization." He raised the shade further. "Man, plenty of cops."

Kelly watched a troop of side-armed, blue-shirted young men in low black boots march toward the front of the train. Czech police, she thought. But there were other not so young men—several pairs of them, in crisp khaki jackets—on the wide platform as well. They inspected the train's sides slowly, bending to peer under the cars. As if someone would be hanging there like in a James Bond film, Kelly thought. The Egyptian? A sad paranoia about Muslims was everywhere. She and Adam agreed on that—plane travel felt more troublesome every trip, "security" making them feel more anxious than secure. They both liked Europe's trains, though this one proved less fancy than the ones they'd ridden in France on their honeymoon. She smiled and pulled the shade down, turned to Adam and, remembering the luxury, hugged him. "We'll be in Vienna soon. Mozart. Sacher tortes. And more palaces for you to dream on," she whispered.

He looked at her with amusement, bent and kissed her, then sniffed. "And a hot bath for you, Mrs. Downey, and a soft towel, and softer bed." He turned on a brighter light, checked his stubble in the compartment's tiny mirror, and prepared his electric razor.

"You think you can go back to sleep when this stop is over?" he asked as the shaver buzzed.

Kelly shoved the upper berth so it locked into place. She sat on the lower and exercised her neck into some semblance of normalcy. She was grateful Adam had booked a hotel for early check-in. He seemed breezy for 4:15 in the morning. They were almost to Vienna, gateway to Europe, where in 1683 the Turks had been turned back, though thousands of immigrants lived there today. He'd told her the story a hundred times. And then there'd be Northern Italy and its idealized romance—Florence, Venice—before a flight to Warsaw to catch their return. She stretched her neck again. Why did she always need to see to the ends of things?

Adam seemed intent, touching up his sideburns with one of her plastic razors over the tiny sink. She took a long drink from their water bottle, and had to pee again. She touched his shoulder and pointed to the door. "They'll be coming. Have the tickets ready."

He put the razor down and tugged on her robe. "One more feel, baby?"

Kelly gasped, turned, and pushed at the door. She fumbled with the locks as Adam chuckled behind her. She left the door swinging as she stepped to the side of the corridor, her image angry and flustered in the distorting glass. She grabbed a rail bar and felt sick to her stomach though there was no motion. She heard the lock click behind her and looked both ways.

At the far end of the corridor, two uniformed officers and two khakied agents had entered the car. Kelly considered returning to the compartment but didn't want to deal with either this hassle or Adam's childish lusts. She paced to the toilet but cringed when she saw its little sign reading "occupied." She looked again as the guard pairs knocked on doors. She trembled, perturbed and somehow guilty. She took a deep breath and dared knock on the bathroom's door to encourage her fellow passenger to hurry up.

"Occupied," a masculine voice said. The Egyptian's tone was no longer friendly but as anxious as her own voice must have sounded to him earlier.

She stepped back to the door and directed her voice to him. "It's me, the woman from the corridor." She thought she could hear his breathing. "Please, hurry."

The door cracked open. He was clothed rather shabbily, she could see in the brightness. A beaten backpack sat beside the metal toilet. His dark face had less color in the metallic light. "What do you want?" he said. He opened the door but hesitated to look further out. "They are coming?" He grabbed her hand and pulled her inside.

Kelly almost cried out, but instead whispered, "The police? Yes." She pressed her back against the wall and tried to signal him out to the four-foot square of platform hidden from the corridor. She pointed at the toilet. "After that I'll help you," she said, hoping to look desperate.

"I will not hurt you." The man closed the door and his face seemed perplexed. "You travel with your … husband … yes?"

"Yes," she said, "with my husband." She fidgeted. "But I have to …" She pointed again to the toilet.

The man sighed but opened the door and peeked to the corridor again. "Hurry," he said as he stepped out. "Please."

Kelly tried to be quick but found herself fumbling. What was she doing? She sat and strained. She heard breathing just outside and realized he had not fully shut her in. The rail yard clamor and pulse of the resting engine made a kind of adagio that troubled the atmosphere. She finished and flushed and began to wash her hands when in the mirror she saw him behind her.

"Keep door locked," he said. "They knock, tell them to talk to your man—you are sick."

Kelly nodded. She put on a look of concern, or was it promise? Why shouldn't she do it, lie for him? The man, an oppressed émigré, had proven no danger to her, just another passenger of the night. Heading where? Any place new, she thought, anything new.

The man looked relieved, averted his eyes, and stepped to the furthest corner of the small room. "Thank you," he murmured. "Al-lah akhbar."

Kelly wanted to touch his arm, to comfort. Instead she whispered, "Where are you from?" She stepped to the door and put her ear against it—only the echoes of the station. "What is your name?" She turned back to him.

"I am Farouk." He looked at her as if seeking understanding. "From Libya. I make a long journey, for freedom."

Kelly smiled. "Farouk, I am Kelly." She offered her hand. "I'm on a journey, too." She felt dishonest. "As a tourist," she added.

Farouk took her hand for only a moment as if it were a forbidden act then stretched against the wall. "When I get to Italy, I will pretend to be tourist, too." He smiled. "My friends will say it." He sighed and looked at the door. "Thank you for helping me."

She touched his arm and his body tensed. He was a fugitive, but she wanted connection, not thanks. "What gave you the courage to leave?"

"Not courage—*al-Qadar*, fate Allah has willed." He looked at her. "I wait for my chance and go."

Kelly leaned against him and he frowned. Voices sounded in the corridor and he pulled away.

A sharp triad of knocks chilled her. "Border Security," called a stern voice.

Kelly measured her distance from the door and loudly said, "I'm busy, please. Compartment 315. Mrs. Downey. Kelly Downey." She held her breath. Farouk's eyes were closed, his face a grimace.

"We will need to see you, madam, in person," the voice commanded. "Please, now."

Kelly took a deep breath. Farouk seemed to be holding his, praying. "All right. One second."

She mussed her hair and loosened her robe, pulling its top open enough to expose a bit of décolletage. As Farouk pressed himself against the wall hidden beside the door, Kelly turned the lock and stuck her face into the narrow space. "It's me," she said, opening the door a bit wider to show her dishevelment.

The agents smiled, and the older one who held her passport chuckled as his eyes inspected her up and down. He checked the photo again, trying to look serious, then closed the little blue book. "Indeed it is you, madam. I shall return your passport to the conductor."

Both agents bowed and turned sharply. Kelly listened to their steps across the platform to the next car before she closed and locked the door.

Farouk still hugged the wall, his breaths rapid. His eyes opened shocked like a man awakened from the dead. "Thank you, thank you." He held his hands folded before him as if praying to her. At the sink he splashed cold water on his face, rinsing his eyes, cooling his neck. "You have saved me." He caught her eyes in the mirror and offered a grim smile. "I will pray for you, that your life be blessed." He lowered his head as he passed her and opened the door. "I will remember you, miss, Kelly, your help."

Kelly put both hands on his arm in light restraint, wanting to touch, something more. But he shook off her hands, his eyes far away. "No. I must not wait now," he said. "*Kon qawiyyan.* Be strong," he commanded." He slid into the corridor, left the door swinging behind him.

Returned to their compartment cleansed, Kelly dressed alone while Adam availed himself of the bathroom. She wondered what he smelled there, if scents lingered in the compressed air—incense, fear, desire—but doubted that Adam would question anything. She pulled on her shoes, but when she stood her head lightened and eyes blurred. Was the world spinning around her?

Shouts and footfalls sounded outside the car. Kelly caught her breath then opened the shade. Yards away on the platform two agents and several of the blue-shirted police surrounded Farouk, who talked rapidly, his uncuffed hands raised. The frozen faces of the officers and the smirks on the agents confirmed that his words were wasted. She stood away from the window and surveyed the little room, searching for a weapon, for anything.

The train jerked forward and Kelly saw a phalanx of men walk Farouk toward the station. He did not resist, but turned his head toward the train several times, his future disappearing. The train rolled and she saw only his profile, but thought she saw some acceptance of fate. She prayed—to Christ and to Allah—that he still had some spark of hope. He deserved his freedom. What future had she earned? "Be strong," she said out loud as the train left the platform, trying to remember the Arabic words as if they could send special power.

She wanted out of the tight room but Adam pulled the door open and stood there, fresh-shirted and shiny-faced. He grinned. "Rarin' to go, Kelly?"

She pushed against him, but he wrapped his arms around her. "Baby, all that crap outside upset you?"

Kelly let herself rest against his chest. Yes, yes, I need to help him, she wanted to shout.

"They caught some Arab guy with no papers. Probably some tool of Mubarak or Qaddafi on the lam."

She threw off Adam's arms and tried not to shake as the train picked up speed. Who knew what was true—brave emigrant or fearful escapee? With the center of his world dismantled, did it matter?

Kelly looked in the mirror at her face, white and frantic. Adam's hands gripped her hips. "You look fine. Let's just sit and relax. They'll bring coffee. We'll be in Vienna in an hour."

She imagined Farouk kneeling in a cell, praying again for his chance. She flashed on the messy lower berth where Adam sat, intent on the Austrian countryside in the soft dawn light.

They were on a night train, heading toward a civilized city, a secure future. It was nearly morning. She would wait for her chance. In Vienna, Florence, Venice, Warsaw. She folded the duvet and sheet, stowed them against the wall and sat down, her shoulder against Adam's until he leaned away. The fields and forests flickered by. A bump threw her against him. She pulled away. Her chance would come. The train's roll pushed her back again. She prayed. And she waited.

———••———

KLEZMER MUSIC

IN THE HOTEL DAVID'S BREAKFAST ROOM, Arne Lindseth loaded a plate from the spread of sliced meats and cheeses, fruits and pastries, touristy scrambled eggs and barely browned potatoes. A British couple muttered complaints, backed by an out-of-place Sinatra serenade, Arne's father's favorite. Three stylish older women—French?—pecked at their small plates. At a back table a man and woman watched the door. Beside them, two boys frowned under snazzy blue yarmulkes. Arne, without the protection of parent, wife, or child, nodded to all as he settled himself near the coffee station. He had only Dara's worn Krakow guide book to pretend to read while he surveyed the diverse crowd.

A klezmer tune, Dara's adopted passion, lilted the guests awake. Was the peculiar sound part of her attempt to acclimate him to Krakow's historic Jewish district, Kazimierz? Dara, his editor and former fiancé booked him here, tucked away from the city's city center and suburbs where he'd interview the modern Poles Dara suggested he survey for his article about the nation's political climate, newly regressive especially when it came to negative history. Klezmer, born ages ago among eastern Europe's Ashkenazi Jews and nearly destroyed like most of Poland's Jews in the Holocaust, was again in vogue around the world. Whatever Dara's intention, Arne felt like a trespasser on foreign turf.

The Jewish man in the corner stood and spoke loudly in the familiar accent of northside Chicago. "I'm sick and tired of her 'acting out'." He glared at his wife. "She's had it!" The woman slumped in her chair and the yarmulked boys' eyes widened. "I will *not* let her ruin another day of this trip with her bad attitude. We're going without her!"

The man, Arne's own age, late thirties, urged his wife from her seat and the boys followed. At the door, she cast a look of apology across the room. Practiced, Arne thought, remembering his own father's Chief Petty Officer's demanding temperament. Glad not to have parental duties himself, he went back to eating, the room quieter than before, Sinatra replacing the klezmer, invoking an old ennui.

Arne layered pieces of cheese, egg, and, yes, ham, onto a muffin. He tried to read a dog-eared description of Auschwitz in the "Sites Nearby" section, but such history wore uneasily on an empty stomach.

A young woman in capri pants and t-shirt entered and panned the room just as Arne took too large a bite. She grinned. His eyes dropped to the book but looked up again when she pulled out the chair from across his table and set down a glass of orange juice.

"Okay?" Her patchouli wafted around her. A plate piled with eggs and sausage topped by a huge sweet roll joined the juice. Arne smiled at her youthful appetite. Her dark eyes reminded him of Dara's—could be her younger sister, or even daughter. She raised thick eyebrows. "Looked like you could use some company."

He chuckled. "Sure, I was missing Chicago." A teenager might appreciate sarcasm. He shoveled down another bite of his muffin concoction.

She seemed to size him up. "Chicago, yes. But Americans? I was tired of them even before we got here, and they're everywhere." She tapped his guidebook with a slender finger. "Even you. I thought maybe you were Swedish, or at worst German—met one of them yesterday." She bit into the sweet roll. "German Jews—a whole bus load of 'em." She raised her eyebrows again. "Who'd'a thunk there were any left?" Arne coughed at her lack of political correctness, but she answered her own question. "Not me. I barely know what I'm doing here myself."

Arne related as she spun her story. The controlling dad had "dragged" the family to the "fatherland" to explore their past, Holocaust tourism one of Poland's thriving industries. She'd escaped most of the Warsaw sites, hanging out in cafés, dad's protests overruled by her mother's accommodation of teenage angst.

Arne explained that he was there writing a piece for *The Chicagoan*—and the city's huge Polish-descended population—about the Polish government's recent turn right, anti-immigration and touchy about retaining its identity despite its membership in the European Union. He watched for an impressed response but got only her chewing. "I'm Arne, by the way. Norwegian-American. Saw your father here a few minutes ago."

The girl groaned. "And still you're able to keep food down." She swallowed and smiled. "I'm Marti and even if you are American, I'm glad to meet a *congenial* older man."

Arne supposed that by comparison he qualified. But Dara hadn't found him so harmonious since he disappointed her with his avoidance of commitment. The minute she'd brought up the subject of children, he returned to his lifelong escape of wandering. Which brought him here, trying to remain … congenial. "Well, at least you have company in your misery. Those boys are your brothers?"

Marti groaned. "My torment. They're finally rooming with Dad." After several nights babysitting them in Warsaw, here she shared a room with her mother. The boys actually looked forward to their visit the next day to Auschwitz. "We are to understand the awful truths all around us here, my father says. My brothers eat it up—war and horror all at once."

The girl's spunk made Arne smile. "Everyone's history's important," Arne said. "Like they say, the truth will set you free."

"Yeah, but at Auschwitz the sign claims it's *work* that makes you free. How'd that turn out? I had enough truth the one time he towed me to the Holocaust Center in Skokie. As if Skokie didn't feel like a concentration camp itself." She drummed her fingers. "Truth is I'm bored to death by death." She sawed at the sweet roll. "I'd much rather soak in café culture than the Schindler Factory. We watched the movie—twice. If I don't fight for it, my life's not my own. It's my father's."

Arne chuckled. He was glad to be past his own father issues, past the conditions and commands. "You're clearly one stubborn girl. No wonder your dad wants to keep an eye on you." He glanced toward the door.

"Oh, he doesn't really. I was a mistake from the beginning. Unexpected, and a girl." Her eyes darted down then back to Arne. "But here I am, damsel not in the least distress."

"But you can't really like being alone in a strange place?" It was time to send her home, even to a careless father.

"You're very observant, Arne. You should take me with you while you research." She winked. "I can be yours for a yes." She took a bite of sweet roll.

In another life Arne might have risked discovering where a 'yes' would lead—not sex with a girl so young, of course, but some curious jaunt around the city. "No, I work alone, Marti. It's think work, not talk work."

She swallowed. "Is it the t-shirt?" She leaned back. "Seventeen ... Will ... Prevail" stretched across her chest. "I clean up nicely, you know." She rose. "But I guess you'll never see." She fluttered her fingers. "See you around, mister, maybe."

And his fledgling comrade was gone.

Arne wandered nearby Szeroka Street, an elongated market square all restaurants, gift shops, and music clubs. Electric tour-mobiles hummed by advertising "Jewish Sites." Arne couldn't imagine Dara suffering this schmaltz but memories from her solo visit three years ago led to the magazine assignment for him. The tourism business was booming, even amid the more repressive politics. There were only 30,000 Jews living in Poland today—down from 3.5 million pre-World War II—but Stars of David promoted kosher menus on every restaurant front in Kazimierz. And such sightseers! Three groups trooped the square. One contained teenagers like Marti gathered around a bronze marker begging visitors to meditate on genocide. Another, black-coated orthodox, followed a dramatic rabbi. The third group, speaking German, pointed fingers and cameras. Somehow, all these folks looked lost though exactly where they meant to be—a center of historic suffering.

He ordered a cappuccino to go at the Café Ester while the Germans scooted chairs on the cobblestone terrace. He considered hiring one of the electric carts to brush up on the historic city, but he could get that stuff from the guidebook. Another part of him wanted to linger, hoping that Marti would chance by and return the joy of journeying to him.

But if he'd learned one thing from travel—girls in trouble are trouble. Especially sweet ones with a sense of irony who wanted something from him. He'd long ago stopped indulging such offers, even innocent ones like Marti's, some urge toward permanence surfacing. But nothing had stuck since he and Dara split a year ago. Arne retreated into stoic melancholy, but Dara suffered the break with good humor. She sent him off on stories, welcomed him back with hugs. Did she still imagine a future together? The future he'd fallen into foresaw only wandering. He counted his change and climbed into a taxi.

His cab veered to avoid one of the tour carts and honked. *"Kretynie!"* his driver shouted. *"Żydzi—Jews—proszę pana.* Everywhere."

Arne shook his head so the driver would log his disapproval. Dara had pointed out how anti-Semitic some Poles seemed, supporting the perception that the Catholic majority had abandoned their neighbors to the ghettos, then the camps. The driver snorted, and revved the engine so the Citröen rattled exhaust into the square. "To where?" he asked without apology.

Arne named a suburban complex of sports fields, mall, Mc-Donald's and KFC, condos, and a sparkling office tower. He'd already settled on contrasting the image of westernizing Poland with the return to reactionary politics. In Chicago, Polish-Americans, Jewish like Dara or not, seemed appalled, or maybe Dara was just projecting. Marti's father seemed not to mind. The cab veered onto a broader street lined with lindens to hide a brick-walled factory. Signs broadcast the tourist sites—Schindler's Factory, Galicia Jewish Museum, Centre for Jewish Culture. Here in the heart of Kazimierz, it looked like 1938, if only the golf carts, signs, and tourists would disappear.

Ahead, a young woman in a honey-colored peasant skirt strolled, checking a phone, licking a gelato cone. Pistachio green glistened on Marti's lip. Arne hoped she was searching for her family but knew better. "Honk please, *proszę,* stop," he said, his phrasebook Polish failing him. He worked the window handle to shout a greeting, but the taxi sped by her.

When Arne returned to Kazimierz that evening, his hotel room felt like a refuge. Around the mall, the people, young ones especially, seemed fully integrated into suburbia. In the central city square, the Rynek, a huge banner from the city government proclaimed, "The Future Started Yesterday," now his article's working title.

Arne half-napped, thinking about the hazelnut torte he'd savored at Café Jama Michalika, double-asterisked by Dara in his guide book. It would have been more fun to watch Marti devour it. Had he become a soft touch for friendship? His short marriage in his twenties had produced no kids, thank God. His involvement with Dara was now over a year dormant. His seagoing father was dead for a decade and his mother warehoused in the maze of Alzheimer's. His distant younger brother, entrenched with his own family, struggled to explain Arne's wanderlust to his children. Arne no longer saw glamour or danger in his freedom. Only the writing gave it a patina of purpose.

Paper crunched under the door. Could it be a note from Marti? Instead, one flier offered a Penderecki concert at Saints Peter and Paul, and another klezmer music at both the Klezmer Hois and Ariel, promising lively sounds to drink to.

He opened a curtain. Dusk's slanting light caught uneven rows of tombstones stretching out beyond a brick wall only twenty yards behind his building. Worn Stars of David showed on a few aged stones, Hebrew lettering on others. Among a copse of yews, the back of the synagogue shadowed the limestone stillness.

He reminded himself he remained jetlagged from the Chicago to Warsaw flight, rumpled from yesterday's train ride to Krakow, still confused by the alleys of old Kazimierz, the destroyed ghetto reclaimed as café culture for tourists. Was some personal reclamation what Dara expected him to find here along with his story?

He dropped her an email. "Thanks for booking this room—sleeping like the dead." She'd probably stayed in this very room on her last trip to Poland, what became her own "Holocaust Holiday." She'd returned more serious, pressing him for marriage, for children. Before, he'd heard her tell a story from her first visit to her great grandparents' fatherland as a college senior. How her cynical friend enjoyed an unexpectedly fantastic pizza, Chicago-style, in Oświęcim, the town hosting the Auschwitz camp. The story always produced nervous laughter, but Dara hadn't told that story since her last sobering trip. A rabbi she'd contacted upon return had reminded her that she could not be a "lapsed Jew," but would always be Jewish, if secular, because a people is defined by more than mere religion. Arne remembered Marti's brothers' yarmulkes and wondered how she resisted the pressure. He could no more see Marti covered by tichel or scarf than himself in a sailor's uniform.

He walked through mist to find food and what he hoped would be fun, even without company. At Miodova, Arne ordered the hearty tomato soup Dara mentioned, and through a bilingual guest requested the recipe. "Just tomato soup," he was told. He dropped by the adjacent Klezmer Hois for dessert and music. "Please go there," Dara had written. "*Real* Klezmer," confirming the outside's sign promise.

The band was playing for only another half hour. A snare drum, bass, violin, accordion, and clarinet belted out tunes, the bassist sometimes singing with a Polish accent in a precise, memorized Yiddish. The musicians were young except the clarinetist, a wiry man in a stiff black suit whose eyes closed as he swung his instrument in arcs with the rhythm. Arne sipped tea and picked at a crumbly cake, keeping time as the music got wilder. From what Dara told him, klezmer music, born of traveling cantors influenced by gypsies, became dance music that mimicked the human voice, its laughter and weeping. Klezmer was the "father of our collective soul," she'd told him. He wondered if Marti's father encouraged this part of their background, the celebration of life, not just the dark history.

Midtune, the clarinetist stood, twirled, then blared a wistful run of discordant flats that climbed high then dropped to a lower range for a final somber passage, the jubilation slowing into elegy. One by one, the younger members stopped playing as the man's last deep notes resonated, each a long, wailing breath. The crowd's heads bowed, cups descended to tables, and Arne bowed in something like a prayer.

Outside, the drizzle had ended. Arne stepped by empty patios until the Ariel, where a boardwalk sign promised klezmer until eleven. He found a seat with a view of stage and crowd, wiped away the sparkle of rain and settled in, debating how vodka would mix with tomato soup and tea. A waitress brought water and a menu but before he could ask for a drink, the chair beside him creaked and patchouli wafted him aware.

"Hey, mister, what are we drinking?"

Marti patted his hand as she sat. The waitress coughed and he ordered a Żubrówka, a sturdy buffalo-grass-flavored vodka. "Marti, for you?" he asked.

The waitress interrupted. "American? Too young to drink here."

Arne pressed Marti's hand to the table. "What, my daughter? Oh, then bring *me* a second drink, please, *pani*. And another water."

The waitress frowned and walked away.

"Hey, thanks, 'Daddy'!" Marti leaned into him. "I knew you'd be up for some cheap thrills after a long day working." She beamed and unzipped a light jacket that covered the peasant dress. "And I do mean cheap. I've passed the whole day on ten bucks my mom sneaked me. But I'm broke now, just to warn you." She shivered in the dampness.

"You should zip that," Arne said. "Does your father let you drink?"

Marti raised her eyebrows. "No, but I do. More like, I drive *him* to drink. And today he'd've let me starve." She ran a finger down the menu. "Promised I'd stay in but wandered around all day. Two ice creams, cup of tea, barley soup, whatever that is. You buying?"

"Sure. At least you had a big breakfast." Arne checked the menu for something to nibble. "What do you suppose this *karp po żydowsku* is?"

"Carp, which the Poles love, and my dad made me eat," Marti offered smartly. "And *żydowsku* means Jewish. I've seen that word more than I can stand." He should have figured it out. "Just get me some pierogi or whatever, please. I've got to text my mother so she can calm the old man. I'll tell her not to wait up."

Her situation hardly seemed dire. The waitress returned and Arne ordered the pierogi, and chicken and beef dishes labeled as *żydowsku*. Dara would enjoy the food photos he'd post on Facebook, maybe even one of Marti that noted their resemblance. He sipped the aromatic vodka. Marti put up her phone and he slid the second glass toward her. "This'll warm you up."

She sniffed the rim before taking a tiny sip. "Empty stomach."

Marti told him about her family's sojourn to every Jewish site in Warsaw. The capital had lots of new cars but no place to park. Mostly she griped about her father's endless history lessons and how the third day she escaped to Old Town's shops and cafés where, even text-leashed to her mother, she felt freedom. "Like now, with you, Arne." She took a slug of the vodka and grimaced. How much freedom was enough. Did any parent ever get that right?

Arne looked around the plaza. No hulking father coming to confront his motives, drag the girl away. The food arrived and he ordered himself another drink while Marti dug in before he could snap any shots.

The group he'd heard at Klezmer Hois set up under the Ariel's awning, minus the old clarinetist but now with a guitarist, the solitary drum replaced by an ill-boding trap set. The young men now wore jeans and t-shirts. Several couples, groups of seemingly local youths, and a half-dozen German tourists took seats.

The bass and guitar offered a familiar rhythm, the accordion adding a klezmer-like riff, but Arne recognized the tune as "Volare." The violinist hammered up the chorus with long shrill notes for "Vo … la … re …" to which the accordion answered "oh, oh" like a circus organ.

Marti nodded toward the band. "*That's* klezmer music? Not what my father described."

"More like klezmer turned plastic." Sacrilege, Dara would say.

A table of young people bounced with the beat. Marti winced. Most youths were miserable, she claimed, trapped by parents' expectations, their futures certain to fall short. Arne remembered wanting only to escape his dad's uneven presence but persistent orders. He'd gone east to school, traveled, and settled in Chicago, two thirds of a continent away from his father's last basing in San Diego, breaking the chain of Viking ancestry, nowhere near an ocean. His father had rarely asked after him.

Now his life seemed one long fugue state, summed up by this trip. Sitting with a girl who might be the daughter he'd never have, listening to artificial music in a city that both denied and sold its past. And brought here by what? An ill-bred distaste for stability and a broken romance with curious strings attached.

Marti finished a last bite, downed her vodka then poured some of his into her glass. "My dad likes this old-fashioned stuff. Catchy." She shimmied her shoulders. "Wanna dance?"

Arne smiled at her determination. He wished he were younger, no, older if also wiser. She sought refuge she was too proud to admit. What else she might think she wanted, he let slide.

"So I guess we'll just sit here." She frowned and watched the band.

Arne explained that every time his father's ship came in he'd cue through his collection of big band tunes. The music passed down by Arne's grandfather grounded the sailor more than land, or family. He'd bored Arne to death, but the records' jaunty rhythms had worked into him.

Another hokey "oh, oh" escaped the accordion. Marti stretched back, her hair falling toward him. Her narrow shoulders rose and collapsed as she breathed. He reached to settle her.

She crinkled her neck. "Oh, a massage. Yes, please." She exaggerated her stiffness.

Arne squeezed twice, his thumbs tracing her wings, then pulled back as the band finished the song with none of klezmer's joyful depth.

"You stopped before you started." Marti scooted to face him and scrutinized his hands.

"Never on Sunday" began like a sodden dirge and Marti raised her eyebrows. The crowd got louder, drinking more. Arne felt a little drunk himself, cheered despite the silly tune.

Marti wriggled and took another slug of the vodka. What would her father think of Arne letting her drink? She giggled and covered his hand with hers until he shook it away. How could a father let his daughter disappear for even a day, texting Mom or not? The man's wish to pass on their heritage meant he hadn't given up on her, but it appeared clear he was losing her, for more than an evening. Arne scanned the square. Why wasn't the place crawling with cops?

The band picked up the pace, the old movie tune merry with both welcome and warning. "You can kiss me on a Monday ...." Marti sang along and swayed, patchouli in the air. "But never on Sunday. Hey, it's not Sunday, Arne."

The violin screeched like a worn needle on vinyl. At the next table the youthful group held hands, did a "wave," then drew on glasses of beer, followed with vodka shots. "The woman in the movie was a prostitute," he informed her. "No great role model." He scanned the crowd. There were probably hookers casing the touristy district right now.

"Why not?" Marti asked. "Maybe I could make it big here." She tossed her hair back and expanded her chest. "Lovely young Jewess working the Holocaust crowd in Poland. I bet there'd be lots of takers." She glanced around. "If not present company."

Arne wanted to slap the foolishness out of her, but her face saddened. Really, he should slap her father. "The phrase is 'present company excepted.' And, Marti, you'd be kidnapped and sold the night you started." He pushed his glass away. "That business is no joke."

The music ended. Marti frowned as she watched the band prepare another foray. Arne wondered what would be next—from the music and from Marti. He threw back his vodka and waved for the bill to cash out before things got even more complicated.

"Get me another one, too?" She sounded young again. "This music is killing me."

"Haven't you had enough, both band and booze?" Though she didn't seem drunk, he needed to send her home, to her father. But that thought made him cringe.

"I've had enough of nothing but all things old," she fired back, accusing Arne. She twisted toward the stage. Unless he dragged her, she wouldn't head for the hotel.

Arne ordered more vodka, one only. A sixtyish man chatted with the band, gesturing toward the microphone stand. Though heavy, he moved crisply in a white suit, shirt open to reveal a gold medallion amid wisps of white chest hair. The group struck up "Are You Lonesome Tonight?" and he began to dance, hips leading the rest of his body in a Polish rumba.

Marti slapped the table. "Now that my dad would *not* do. Dancing's too freeing."

"I saw your father this morning—he's not nearly that heavy."

She shrugged. "True, but just as embarrassing."

"Fathers can be like that," Arne said, remembering his own father's lapses into public command-giving. "And this guy's probably someone's dad himself, so be kind."

The man strutted onto the patch of pavement serving as dance floor. Some young women giggled as he repeated the melancholy lyrics. His voice wasn't bad. He held out a meaty hand and one woman in a summery dress rose. He swirled her a few turns before singing again, more breathlessly. When she sat down he knelt and serenaded the final words to her. "Tell me dear, are you lonesome tonight?" She gifted him a flower from a vase on the table.

Marti frowned. "I might as well admit it, Arne. I am lonesome." She tilted her head and touched his hand. "Can't I stay with you, just tonight? I'll sleep on the floor."

Arne debated her neediness. "Impossible, Marti, and you know it." He pulled free of her. "Your father, bad as you think he is, needs to know you're safe." Around the square, lights glowed in the mist. There was more he wanted to say. "I've got a thing or two to tell him. I actually hoped he'd show up looking for you."

Marti grimaced. "Shows what you know." She jerked away, back to the band. "He's trying to make me need him." She threw her head back. "I don't *need* anyone, mister."

The big man, beaming at the applause, upped the stakes with "Bésame Mucho." He crooned in accented English, probably learned from the Elvis recording. "Kiss me as if this night was our last time."

Arne groaned, but Marti puckered her lips. "Kiss me many times," she sang softly.

The man went on, wide-eyed. "Because I'm afraid to lose you." He spun away from the women's table.

Marti bent forward, her hair brushing Arne's hands on the table. "Just like my father, making a fool of himself."

The waitress placed the fresh vodka in front of Arne, asked if they wanted dessert. He considered whether a sweet bribe would settle Marti's hunger, but signaled they were fine.

Marti scooted her chair close again and grabbed the glass as if it were an unopened present. The singer changed back to the original Spanish, *"Bésame, bésame mucho,"* in a dramatic tremolo that Marti mocked.

Arne put a finger to his lips to quiet her. "If history has it right, that song was written by a Mexican girl about your age—15? Claimed she'd never been kissed."

Marti leaned closer to him. "I'm 17 and I've been kissed plenty, mister." She threw her arms around his neck and pressed her lips against his even as he grabbed her arms to force her away.

Her wrists felt thin in his hands, and she tugged free and leaned back. But there was no joy in his successful defense. Why *should* she know what she wanted? He'd mistaken other needs for romance more than once while wandering. And back home, why did he hold onto his drama with Dara?

"Marti, I'm sorry life's so confusing." Arne felt himself condescending as the fat man sang a verse in Polish. "It confuses us all."

"I really like you, Arne." Marti stood. "You treat me like an adult." She emptied the glass. "Well, more or less."

Marti danced toward the singing man as Arne gripped the arms of his chair. The old man sang, "Hold me, my darling." She offered herself and the man took her in one arm and twirled, encouraged her body to fall back as if swooning. She played along, hand fanning her face but, from between her fingers, her gaze settled on Arne.

The big man drew her close and pursed his lips with another

"bésame." Arne shuddered and prayed she wouldn't do it. But Marti greeted his lips with an obviously open mouth. The women at the table laughed and the man lit red with excitement. He kissed her back, hard, and held tight when Marti struggled to pull away.

As Arne stood and took a step toward them, the singer let her go. The man seemed puzzled, measuring her slim build and age, embarrassed, his flight into fantasy not worth Arne's punishment. Marti was blushing and puffy-eyed but managed to curtsy before she fled into the square.

The waitress called to Arne, "Must pay, for the music also." He threw several large bills onto the table so she'd see he was no criminal. He tramped away in the direction Marti had taken, up Szeroka toward the synagogue. But parked cars made him shift off the sidewalk, and uneven cobblestones slowed his pace. By the time he reached the square's end, she had disappeared. He stood alone in the renewed drizzle.

Arne caught his breath and looked back. The hotel, and sleep, waited a block away. He pictured Marti as he'd seen her on the street that morning, free, enjoying gelato … and alone, heading where? He quick-stepped to the cemetery's wall and into a streetlamp's glow. A late-returning tour cart hummed by and from some distance he heard a clarinet's wistful tune. Was the old musician playing on the street for coins?

He followed the wall until a yellow bulb lit the synagogue's wrought-iron gates. Marti crouched against the bars like a shadow and he wondered if she'd vomited. He heard her crying.

He knelt and gave her an awkward hug. She sobbed on his shoulder. The clarinet's sweet lament drifted in again. "That's the real klezmer you need to hear, all life's emotions at once." He embraced her, his face against hers, worried suddenly that his evening beard might scratch, but she pressed her cheek back, her breath uneven on his skin.

"You have to go home now." He helped her to her feet. "I'll explain things to your father in the morning. You know he loves you."

Marti shuddered. "My father won't even care I'm back. He only wants to pass down fears. He'll drag me along to Auschwitz tomorrow then guilt me when I don't give a damn." She leaned into the ironwork. "And he won't take your explanation. He'll throw a punch." She searched Arne's face. "Please don't throw one back."

Arne squeezed her hand. "If you'd feel guilty, you must care. Your father wants you to know your past so you can know yourself." Arne remembered stalking out of his parents' house, college bound but heading nowhere, knowing everything except himself. "Your past won't stay behind. Don't confront it and you'll wander through life until you do."

Marti stretched and put her arms around Arne's neck. "I love you, Arne." She kissed his cheek. "You came after me."

He held her until both their hearts calmed.

Arne sat in the breakfast room, drinking too much coffee, waiting for them as smooth pop songs and brooding klezmer alternated moods.

After delivering Marti to her room, he'd watched fog rise over the graveyard's resurrected stones. He'd e-mailed Dara that he'd be visiting Oświęcim, most likely with new Chicago friends, to absorb as best he was able the awful history. He thanked her for the ancient music, its humanity, and her own. He imagined a future together, made her a promise he intended to keep.

———•———

RENATA

1973

THEIR NEW COWORKER TOM SAT SHAKING WITH anger as Renata neared the end of her survival story. Kathy and the other five girls of the Records Entry Unit paid attention to their boss's tale a hundredth time. How in her native Yugoslavia, Renata—"a clerk, like you girls"—had checked in prisoners at the city jail before they were shipped elsewhere. How her Croatian bosses and the German officers who commanded them admired her long dark hair, how they trusted her with black market money and gave her coal for her mother's stove. How, when the war went bad and the Germans abandoned their Ustaše allies, the partisans—Serbians in league with the Soviets threatened to shave off her hair like they did the collaborating prostitutes. Kathy touched her own short hair, imagining the punishment especially hateful to any woman. What Tom made of that horror she read in the glaring eyes framed by his long hippie hair.

Renata went into her closing flourish. The woman—around fifty, Kathy's mother's age if she hadn't died—loosened the bun

44

of her hair and twirled her stocky form so strands swept the air around them. "You see, Tom?" Renata stopped her dance right in front of his boyish bearded face. As she bent her hair flooded over her shoulders and onto her bosom. "I still have my hair. The partisans tried to take it. But I escaped." She straightened and smiled right at him. "And then"—she turned toward Kathy—"I came here to America."

Renata marched away from their work stations, halted and aimed her stern gaze toward them all. "And so you see I will survive even your bumbling, Tom. Now you will be back to work." She focused on Tom. "Do not make the same mistake again."

Her boss could be harsh, but sometimes the other girls did tend toward slacking. Kathy was glad Renata cared enough to want them to do the job well. She was proud to be Renata's liaison to the others, unofficial though the position was. Tom Smith would only be with the unit for two weeks, and the first of those ended today, but he clearly had it in for her boss. Renata's own boss, Dr. Gaunce, the head of Serials Section, was wrapped around Tom's finger, but Renata didn't seem concerned. Kathy had taken her to lunch on Wednesday to warn about Tom's probing questions, but Renata said, "Questions and looks don't kill, Kathy." And even today when Tom asked directly what she'd done in the war—World War II, not Viet Nam—Renata boasted about her roots in Croatia, her escape from communism, her emigration. But even now that Renata *had* answered his question, Kathy knew Tom's distrust wouldn't end.

Periodicals record-keeping was changing, and that was why Tom got his job. Though he was a history major, he knew something about computers, probably because he smoked dope with the engineering students who played Battleship or Pong over telephone lines with geeks a thousand miles away at Stanford and MIT. Or so he said. Kathy had no idea how the modem thing he described worked or why the university allowed dead-of-night gatherings of ne'er-do-wells in the Electrical Engineering labs. Anyway, Tom was smart enough to take notes and communicate with the Library's consultants who logged the holdings information—data, they called it—into machines. Then came "print-outs" of wide green-and-white-striped paper with the journal titles, numbers, and dates in incomplete-looking letters called "dot-matrix." The same information the girls hand-wrote on the cards filling wooden files. The university subscribed to around 10,000 journals, monograph series, and annual editions, so there was plenty to track—hence the half-dozen assistants under Renata's command. Renata was the most senior sergeant in Dr. Gaunce's small company. Tom was assigned to them in Records to learn firsthand what happened when an issue arrived in the mail.

The highfalutin' technicians had finally assigned a useful task— after the new system was half set up! Further changes were coming, but Renata assured Kathy her job was secure, she would be just fine since Renata was on her side. Dr. Gaunce needed Renata, and Renata needed Kathy, her most senior recorder except for Lucille, who was black and so didn't really count.

But gossip about Renata's stern will ran rampant in the professional Cataloguing Unit, perhaps more so since Tom started questioning her life. He was the only male in the entire twenty-person Periodicals Section except for Dr. Gaunce, who'd most likely hired him for relief from the female gender. Getting the job had been easy for Tom—like everything else his whole life, Kathy imagined. Then instead of sticking to his business, in downtimes he'd grilled every one of the girls about Renata's stories—her wartime work in her homeland and her arrival in America.

Now here he was, boring a hole in Renata's back while the girls got to work. If Renata had been one of the younger women, Tom would have been gazing lower. Becky, the new girl with huge breasts, said he creeped her out. But Barb, one of Kathy's co-recorders, thought he was "hippie cute" with his hair grown out from its professional trim at his hiring two months ago. And it couldn't be more obvious that Cindy, the secretary in Cataloguing, had a crush on him even though she'd recently separated from her grad student husband. Today, Cindy'd come in without a bra in a lilac shirt, its top button opened or closed depending on Tom's proximity. Even Dr. Gaunce finally spied the see-through blouse and looked away, embarrassed the rest of the afternoon. Maybe a weapon lay hidden in Tom's shenanigans, if it turned out Kathy needed one to protect Renata.

Instead of driving home, Kathy waited in the parking garage, breathing acrid fumes, hidden by a concrete pillar near the elevator. Cindy parked here, too. Tom had headed toward the wrong elevators if he really walked to work from the second-floor walk-up on Sabol Street he'd rented after graduating. He wouldn't be around town long—he'd mentioned trying graduate school himself, somewhere far away. But lots of his type lingered as the call of adult responsibility bred both fear and resentment of people who had to work for a living, people like Renata and Kathy.

Sure enough, when the lift's doors opened, there were Cindy and Tom, embracing, bodies rubbing, his hand inside that flimsy shirt, and their tongues going at it. The couple didn't break apart until the elevator began to close.

They remained too enrapt with each other to notice as Kathy followed the swerving car to the graduate student garden complex. Cindy parked at a bad angle, then she and Tom sprinted to her front door where she must once have happily greeted her husband.

A few weeks ago Kathy had been in the apartment herself, attending a baby shower for Marie Simon. She'd asked Renata to drive with her, but Renata begged off, too busy to attend. She did toss in $5 for the office gift, an expensive stroller, smiling when she mouthed "another Jewish baby" so only Kathy saw. Tom had been invited too, even though he was a man. In addition to the ten he'd chipped in on the stroller, he brought a blue and pink onesie with the words "Peace Now" in appliqué. Marie went nuts unwrapping it, and kissed Tom on both cheeks.

Now at the door, Tom had one hand up Cindy's skirt and the other teased her breasts. He might be heading toward fatherhood himself. Kathy giggled. Couldn't they wait? Finally Cindy put the key in the lock and they slid inside. Kathy hoped one of the neighbors saw—broad daylight, after all—and made a call to the housing people. Or maybe Kathy herself would call. Or maybe slip an unsigned note to Dr. Gaunce.

She didn't wait around to see how long Tom stayed, or if he spent the night. Kathy's suspicions were confirmed.

The next day, Kathy knocked at Renata's house. Renata's husband Karl from Germany, who lectured in chemical engineering, would be at the football game. So she planned to invite herself in for afternoon tea and report on the new protection Tom's office fling might offer.

Renata paused at the door as if she might not let Kathy in. She rubbed her eyes at the sunshine. "I am tired, Kathy, and napping." For a second her complaint reminded Kathy of her mother. But Renata finally smiled. "You know how when Karl is gone, the house gets quiet. But come in, of course." She expected to hear some feisty spark in Renata's voice. But her boss, her friend, sounded worn out, maybe more worried than she admitted.

Kathy had visited several times, and she and her husband Brad had come for dinner several months ago. But Karl acted a bit imposed upon, and Brad kept his mouth shut but didn't much appreciate Karl's complaints about giving in to the communists in Viet Nam. Losing despite Brad's brave efforts fighting there, of course, Karl added. Even if Brad had liked the better off older couple, Kathy was too embarrassed to invite them to their trailer home.

Renata's home held a kind of dust-filtered elegance. The heavy drapes hung in a rich gold brocade and much of the furniture—a carved wooden chest and an elaborate sideboard "ordered from the old country"—appeared antique. She must have a lot of fine things to store, Kathy thought. She wished her own family, miserably poor, had owned more to pass along than bad memories and "good riddance."

The house held a pungent smell, too, especially in the kitchen when they entered to make the tea, like something burned this morning or the night before. Bacon? And when Renata turned on the burner a bit of grease flickered under the teapot, a clunky metal tomato. Country kitsch seemed plentiful in the room. There were folk-art paintings on the walls, from old women working fields, their heads wrapped in scarves, to pipe-smoking old men in wooden rockers. Near the dining room door, a cuckoo clock hung, not ticking.

"It no longer works," Renata said. She put her hand on Kathy's shoulder. "The singing bird inside has died." She chuckled and went about pouring the water.

"You have wonderful things, Renata, even if they are old." She flushed, hoping Renata didn't think she was referring to Renata herself. "I love your house, so comfortable and safe."

Renata poured honey and milk into both cups without asking. "Old is right, dear Kathy." She passed Kathy a saucer and cup. "But I'm glad you feel safe here." Renata shook her head. "I do not always feel so protected, even in my own little corner of the wide world."

In the living room her boss nodded Kathy into to an overstuffed chair beside the coffee table. Renata sat on the sofa, damask-upholstered with unmatched pillows in chenille patterns and toile landscapes. She set down her saucer and sipped from the cup, her pinky finger extended as if she were a countess.

Kathy sampled the stinging liquid.

"You like the tea? It's minty and fresh, yes? I add sprigs of peppermint from my garden." Renata took a long drink from her own cup and looked right into her. "What is bothering you, Kathy?"

Renata was direct as always. When a young woman began at the job, Renata placed her in a chair and sat beside her, led the girl through the process for a half hour or so, then rose with the words,

"And now you begin, yes," a command, not a question. Frowns, even scowls, showed her impatience with a slacker's error. Kathy herself had been on the receiving end of harsh words over the three years she'd worked there, but she'd learned that obedience earned not only Renata's approval but small rewards—Hershey's Kisses, and once a lacy handkerchief on her birthday. She'd become the right-hand man, so to speak, the corporal in Sergeant Renata Dunkel's squad of clerks.

Still, Kathy didn't know how to return to the issue of Tom's suspicious nature. She kept sipping tea as Renata held her eyes. "Now aren't we friends, Kathy? You tell me what is worrying you."

Kathy looked around the dimly lit room—sunlight sliced the draperies and cut across the coffee table as she put down her cup and saucer. "Renata, I think Tom is after you. He keeps questioning what you've told us about the war, about Yugoslavia, about where you worked, the jail." She released a heavy sigh. "He told Barb you must have worked for the Nazis and should never have been let into the country."

Renata nodded slowly, her round face empty of emotion.

"He's talked to all the girls, I think. And I caught him quizzing Lucille in the break room just Thursday. She was saying, 'My, my, do tell,' like she does about everything." Kathy stirred the air with her hands. "Tom looked really pissed off, irritated, you know, because he couldn't get more reaction out of her."

Renata leaned into the sofa. "Lucille is a steady worker, but stupid. She knows nothing and says nothing worth hearing. That's why she agrees with all you say. 'My, my' is her colored stupidity." Renata glanced at the closed drapes then back to Kathy. "She is a clerk, Kathy, nothing more. And you are more, a friend, for trying to warn me." Renata lifted herself, went to the window, and pulled one drape open. Light flooded into the room.

She turned to Kathy and, despite her flowered dress and apron, looked strong and stern. "Tom knows just enough from history books to think me horrible. But you should not worry, Kathy. You understand who is your ally and who is your enemy. He cannot harm us. I did only what I was told to do." She took a step toward Kathy. "He talks to you girls because he is too afraid to confront me directly." She put her hands on Kathy's shoulders. "Now, let's have another cup of tea. And ginger cookies."

Kathy sat in her modest home, blinds up, sun shining in. She hadn't pushed Renata about what Tom might think was worth knowing beyond what he'd heard in the office. She also hadn't told Renata about Tom and Cindy. The tea and cookies were tasty but Kathy more clearly remembered the kitchen's burnt smell. Should she have offered to help Renata clean?

Football game won, students who lived in nearby trailers were coming home to celebrate with late afternoon grilling. Her Brad would be home soon after another Saturday of overtime at the Chrysler plant, working his way up, like Kathy, slowly but surely, the way everyone said it should be done. She remembered Renata's comment about their friendship and how Kathy was more than a clerk.

And she remembered things Renata told her privately long ago. How, a clerk herself, she'd been promoted from work in a jail in her home city to a close-by labor camp. It wasn't run by the Germans—they left justice to their Croatian allies, the Ustaše. She was only a teenager, younger than Kathy was now, taking names, keeping track of inventory. She went out for bread or coal, or to scrounge up eggs or ham. She knew who to ask and how to demand. She had this power, yes, but also the power of her beauty. She'd known some German officers—near the war's end one of them put her in touch with Karl. She spoke of her will to survive and doing what was necessary. And as she'd told them all, at war's end the Serbs had wanted to cut off her hair and parade her like they did whores. But even partisans were bribable by beauty, and so she escaped to Karl in Germany, and with him to America, her long hair intact. Even fading into gray, Kathy thought, Renata's hair remained beautiful.

Then Brad got home anxious to talk and took her to dinner at their favorite, Ponderosa. He'd had a good day. One of the plant's managers, unhappily working Saturday, said there was no reason Brad couldn't run the damn line himself. "You union guys, especially you veterans, make the trains run on time,'" Brad reported as he chomped his ribeye.

Sunday morning Kathy woke late to sunshine and Brad's satisfied snoring. She scanned the packed bedroom and felt secure. Look what was hers—Brad's love, a comfortable place, a good job, and a whole day off.

She shuffled to the kitchen and made coffee in the brand new Mr. Coffee brewer Brad bought for her birthday a month ago, putting her ahead of their neighbors for once. It made strong coffee, the way they both liked it. Then she remembered Tom bragging that in California last summer he'd bought coffee beans of various "international" types. He'd shared an African blend at the office and, she had to admit, it tasted bitter, but exotic, good.

Maybe Tom'd been places she hadn't but, knowing about Cindy, Kathy could deal with him. She didn't believe he'd be able to hurt Renata badly, but she'd read about war criminals being chased by Israel or rounded up for trial in Europe. Renata was no war criminal, just a clerk—no crime in that! The authorities let her into the country, so her papers must have been in order. Maybe he'd slander her around the library with baseless accusations. She saw from every new clerk's reaction how hard it must be already for Renata, with her harsh accent—"is she German?"—broad build, and expectations of hard work. Even Dr. Gaunce seemed not to really like her, but depended on her to keep the recording a smooth-running accessory to the important business of acquisition and cataloguing.

Outside, the residue of last night's partying dotted the small strips of yard between the trailers. The sun glinted off the beer bottles and pop cans. Stray dogs nosed paper plates littered around overflowing trash cans. Kathy shivered. Brad would want to sleep until noon and then watch pro football. She made sure of cold Stroh's in the fridge and Totino's in the freezer in case her errands kept her out all day. It might take her a while after mass to hunt down Tom and let him know what she'd do if he didn't stop asking so many questions.

And what exactly would she do? She sat in the pew. If God was listening He surely understood that this wasn't vengeance but protecting someone who needed help. It was clear Tom had no morals, hounding the old woman with no forgiveness in his heart. Like the Romans, she thought, like the high priests who took down Jesus.

Kathy stood and sang the Lamb of God then knelt before communion. Okay, so Renata was no Jesus, even though she was being martyred. She knelt and apologized to God, but got no guidance even when she repeated, "say the word and I shall be healed." The communion hymn began and she waited for the usher to direct her up. "Make me a channel of your peace," she sang, anxious to get on with her mission. "Where there is hatred, let me bring your love." She remembered how years ago she'd first heard the words in English, not Latin, and felt guilty for hating her mother. The Church and its rituals were about the only thing she'd held onto from her childhood. She rose and took the host and wine, then stepped around others to the door to be one of the first out.

She smiled at the priest as he shook her hand then left without a word to anyone. Renata deserved the kind of peace the Church promised. She'd suffered plenty to get here. She'd worked hard and didn't expect special favors. Just put her nose to the grindstone and stuck to her own business. If Renata's past included ghosts, they flew between her and God. Not Tom or anyone else. Kathy climbed into her car and, her fingers shaking on the key, turned the ignition on. She gunned the car with a vengeance.

Tom wasn't at his walk-up when she knocked. She climbed back down the steep outdoor steps, smelling the residue of another tenant's breakfast. Burnt toast. The sweet stink of greasy bacon. She was a grapefruit and cereal person herself, though she'd fry up salty food for Brad when he had time to sit for it. Had Tom spent the weekend at Cindy's?

Kathy drove in that direction, eyes on the sidewalks. Little traffic in the student ghetto. Some stumbling home with hangovers or from morning sex with last night's stranger. A sophomore awakened by a nightmare about a paper due on Monday. She giggled. The more serious would be out and about soon, to the library perhaps.

Kathy wondered if Tom might be there, too. All the time he wasted asking questions about Renata or checking out the girls put him behind on his workload. The computerizing process had turned out to be more time-consuming than anyone expected. The technology was full of "glitches," their word for bad ideas and mistakes. Dr. Gaunce himself often worked Sundays, Kathy knew—what a lonely man.

She pulled into the parking garage, glad to be only a clerk, even if it made her happy that Renata thought of her more highly, a bit like a daughter. She parked and walked to the elevator, trying to come up with a good reason to give for checking in on a Sunday. She'd find something around her desk to claim she needed at home. Then ask Tom to help her with a problem with her car. A meeting in the shadowy garage seemed appropriately neutral.

Kathy found the Serials Section's doors locked. She considered leaving, but maybe Tom, being the paranoid type, would be in there alone. Her key turned the heavy bolt and she pushed open the doors into plenty of light, but didn't see Tom anywhere. He might be checking the stacks, she thought, and went to her desk to fiddle around and wait.

She found some Wite-Out she might claim to have needed, but that would be pilfering. She took a little bottle of Midol out of her purse and put it in her drawer—eureka! A noise behind her startled her around. From the doorway of their break room Tom rushed out, saw her, turned red-faced, and headed for his permanent desk over in Cataloguing.

Dr. Gaunce appeared in the lounge doorway, tall and skinny, his hawk-nose shiny with sweat, straightening his clothes. "Oh, it's just you, Kathy," he said, pondering her as if she'd broken the law. "What are you doing here on a Sunday, might I ask?" He drew his gawky body up and craned his neck. He looked like a cartoon vulture.

"I forgot some medicine, Dr. Gaunce." She closed the desk drawer and held up the Midol, making herself blush. "I didn't think there'd be anyone here to bother."

Dr. Gaunce looked over to Tom, who was straightening his desktop, maybe cleaning it out. "I'll be going," Kathy said. "Got to fix Brad's dinner." She walked past Dr. Gaunce to the door. "Sorry to have bothered you." She waved at Tom like they were friends. "See you, Tom," she called brightly as she left their workplace.

Kathy unlocked her car door, her nose stinging at the lingering hint of gasoline. What were those men up to? Who'd been doing what to whom? She laughed and her keyring fell to the concrete floor in a clatter. It didn't really matter, because whatever and whoever, *that* kind of office romance would not be tolerated.

When she stood, Tom was pacing toward her from the elevator. He looked mad enough to kill. "Hold on, Kathy," he commanded.

"What the fuck are you doing here on a Sunday?" His glare cut through her. "It's bad enough Gaunce calls me in to 'tell me an interesting story,' orders me to take it easy on Renata, then makes a pass." He moved between her and the car. "And Renata sends you spying." He grabbed her shoulder. "Isn't that it?"

Kathy pulled away, sorting through his meaning. Then she hiked her knee into his groin.

Tom grimaced and bent over, limped back as she climbed into the car.

"Keep away from me, you perverted freak!"

Instead he leaned toward her. "Wait, Kathy." He thrust his fingers onto the door so she couldn't close it without crushing his hand. "I don't care what you think about me, but why do you want to protect her?" He leaned there huffing, weak as a kitten.

"Why do you hate her? She's just an old woman trying to do her job." Kathy put her legs outside the door. "You're driving her crazy with your bullshit accusations." She smirked and stood up. "And all the time, you playing this freak show with Dr. Gaunce." She took a step toward Tom. "Who'd have thought Mr. Stud Goldilocks was a queer."

Tom shook his head but Kathy knew she had him. "Don't you think they'd want to hear about this little affair, on top of you messing around with Cindy?" She felt her face redden. "What do they call boys like you? Switch-hitters?"

Tom dropped his arms. "No, I'm not, but apparently Gaunce is gay. So, he's weird. What about it, you bigot?" His lips tightened. "You want to sew a pink triangle on him like Renata would? Don't you get it? She was in the Ustaše, a Nazi or good as. Lied about it like her rocket-scientist husband. There are people who should be told!"

Kathy shuddered but stood her ground. She'd looked up the facts when Tom started his questioning. Pink triangles for homosexuals, red ones for communists, black for gypsies, yellow stars of David for Jews. But for the Croatians it was more a civil war. Most of the prisoners Renata dealt with were Serbs—blue badges—Croatia's enemies who wanted to take her hair. Her enemies.

"Renata was just a clerk, Tom. She didn't do those awful things. She wanted to stay alive." Kathy glared at him. "Like all of us, Tom, even you." She enjoyed his confused look. "And if you know what's good for you—and good for Dr. Gaunce—you'll keep your mouth shut about her." She climbed into the car. "For sure she's not hurting anyone now, and I won't let you hurt her."

She closed the door, but when Tom came to the window she rolled it down. He put his hands on the frame and stared. "There's no reason for you to hurt Gaunce," he said. "Or me." He looked at her as if she was the freak. "Her bunch murdered a half million people. All of them were 'just clerks,' Kathy, every one of them, to hear them tell it." He stepped back. "Why do you defend her? What's Renata to you, anyway? She bosses everyone around like slave labor and you're a good German to take it."

Kathy stared at his complacent face, his own long hair. "You don't understand anything, Tom." She tried to look fierce. "She's a human being, and a person that cares about me, that's who."

He kept shaking his head.

"And she told me she was sorry," she lied, for no reason except to end the discussion.

Tom backed off and Kathy rolled up the window and started the car. He stood in the exhaust smoke as she pulled away, staring after her like she was an escaping criminal.

Kathy checked on Brad, deep into his football game with his friend Ricky, both just this side of tipsy. The boys began teasing her and begging snacks, and Kathy decided she'd better leave before they sent her out for more food, beer, or simply to see if they'd get by with it. But at least they had some balls!

Her wipers threw droplets off the windshield. Renata would surely have advice about Tom and Dr. Gaunce, and Kathy hoped two visits in one weekend wouldn't be overdoing their friendship. The light traffic cruised ghostly in the mist, through this town where she'd grown up outside the stream of university students, intellectuals, and more recently protesters for peace. But all that time, she was getting somewhere, bettering herself. The meek *would* inherit the earth, she thought, turning it into a chant to the wipers' beat.

By the time she pulled up at Renata's house the rain had stopped. She sat in the car, watching the curtained windows for any sign of life. Renata was trying to play it cool, but she must feel Tom questioned her very life. Tom wouldn't dare speak now. He'd stay as silent as that house. She wanted Renata to feel the relief she felt. And, yes, tell her about kneeing him in the balls. The look on his cocky face—that was a laugh! She practiced her joke in the visor mirror and touched up her lipstick. Renata was still her boss as well as her friend. She wanted to show respect.

Kathy rang the bell. She surveyed the neighborhood of solid

older houses, tall hardwood trees, well-kept yards. Renata fit well here even if she preferred to hide away. After a minute or two, Kathy rang again, then knocked.

The door opened and Renata stood frowning, wearing an unclosed robe with flimsy nightgown showing, a confused look framed by her flowing hair. "Kathy, what are you doing here, on Sunday?" Renata seemed about to dismiss her. "A day for peace, my dear, not troubles." She glanced back into the dark house. "But come in, come in. Karl is napping." She held her finger to her lips. "So we will speak quietly, yes?"

Renata shuffled across the heavy rugs in slippered feet, turned on one of the lamps, laid Kathy's jacket on the chair's arm, and bade her sit in the same spot as yesterday. "Now, what is going on, Kathy?" She sat on the couch. Her heavy legs showed to the knee and Kathy realized she was wearing hose, the old kind with seams running up the back. Renata reached over and touched her arm. "You are worried, child." Renata's smile wrinkled in dismay. "Are you still losing sleep over our troublesome Tom?"

Kathy's tongue went dry and she wished Renata would offer the pungent tea. She mouthed "yes," but avoided Renata's eyes. "I had a run-in with Tom," she said. "I put him in his place." She looked up for Renata's reaction. "And I found out some things about Dr. Gaunce, too." Renata nodded grimly, understanding her. "I don't think he'll bother you any more, Renata. I'm sure neither of them will."

Renata stood and straightened, looked around the room. "But you see, they have never bothered me, Kathy." She went to the window and pushed the drape aside. "I am quite familiar with the weaknesses of our dear Gaunce. And Tom is nothing, knows nothing about me, about the war. He runs about squealing like a piglet."

Kathy found herself shaking. Renata's words seemed savage.

Renata let the drape fall, a sliver of sunlight beaming in. She turned toward Kathy, stern. "But what has happened?" She took two steps, her pale skin revealed wrinkles beneath the gown. "What have you and the boy been up to?"

Kathy sank into the soft chair. She craved the tea, or even water, and looked toward the kitchen, hoping Renata would take the hint. She didn't want to say more. Enough to say she could protect her friend, that Tom and Gaunce would never bother her.

Renata stepped beside the chair, her odor musky, the fabric of her robe scratching Kathy's arm when she bent. She took Kathy's shoulder in one strong hand, and with the soft fingers of the other guided her chin so Kathy looked up into her face. "Kathy, do not play games. Tom is our enemy in the office, we know. But I did nothing wrong. Ours was a cause."

Renata pinched Kathy's chin. "It is good you too have found a cause, working so hard to stop his torment." She turned toward the window. "He hurts us all with his new computers." She looked again through the drapes. "And his suspicions."

Kathy reached for her jacket on the couch's arm and jostled the lamp. Renata pulled the drapes more tightly closed. Her gown glowed in the lamplight, her face obscured. "Kathy, what have you found out? Perhaps it will be useful." Renata's heavy form swung toward her. "What have they been up to?"

Kathy wanted only to leave. She started to lift herself from the chair, but Renata flanked her movement. Renata took the jacket from Kathy's hands and tossed it onto the couch behind her. Kathy placed her elbows on her knees and let her head fall as Renata's scent, inches away, forced her nostrils closed. She gasped, exhaled a long sigh.

Renata edged closer, smoothed the collar of Kathy's blouse. She tightened her eyes as Renata's fingers spread to cup her chin. "And now, my Kathy, you will tell me all you know."

NITE OWL

THROUGH THE SNOW BLUE NEON GLOWED IN sequence, "Nite" "Owl" "Inn." Andy imagined the bug-eyed cartoon owl crying "Who Who Who," but his real question was "why." Why the hell was he here? A signature—"Ralph's"—flashed red three times then disappeared. Here in Battle Ground, Indiana, he felt anything but a wise owl. He trudged across Railroad Street to the bar's wide door, its windows obscured by glaze. Inside, Caroline supposedly waited. She'd disturbed his evening, not that there was much to interrupt, begging him to drive ten miles from Lafayette through the blizzard into the middle of nowhere. *Now* she needed him. They'd been broken up since June when she'd returned from a trip to San Francisco bent on changing her whole world. She gave him a choice, come with or lose her, but Andy wouldn't commit. The romance they'd settled into their whole senior year became excess baggage for lives booked to travel different directions.

A kick from his wet cowboy boot blasted snow into the air. Caroline liked the boots, his jeans, his father's old peace sign belt-buckle, his lean solid body—all reasons why she still called whenever she'd worked her small self into big trouble. She might deny it, but at heart she missed his stoic embracement of his roots.

He pulled the door open, the wind drawing out a cloud of cigarette smoke. He stepped into the barroom greeted by shouts of "close the fucking door" from a table of card-players frozen mid-hand by the gust. Andy pulled the door closed and the frowning men turned back to their game beneath colorful crepe paper streamers and a banner blaring "Mardi Gras."

Andy shook the snow from his duster and tramped to the bar. Caroline sat on a stool beside a small guy with bleached hair. Her animated gestures suggested she was giving him a lecture. Another much larger red-headed man stood behind the blond, waiting to order, peering at Caroline as if he'd like to rip the words from her pretty mouth—no doubt the troublesome guy she'd called him about. She ignored the big man but noticed Andy and waved him over, her face tinted by blue bar light.

"Hey ya, stranger!" She rose from the stool and spread her arms to hug him. She whispered, "I've got things under control now, thank God." She kissed near his ear. "Sorry to bring you out into this." She patted the empty stool to her left. "Let me buy you a drink."

Andy draped his long coat over the stool and sat. He nodded to the blond guy then at the big man who kept staring. Caroline and the tanned guy seemed out of place here—a petite well-dressed blond and the guy small town bar boys might call girly, meaning not quite gay, or maybe. Between Caroline's lecture and the tough guy's glare, Andy related.

"Andy, this is Gene." The guy with big brown eyes and long lashes grinned. "We met in San Francisco and he's come out to visit." She hadn't mentioned Gene in her plea for rescue. "To say the least, he's had an interesting introduction to our home state." She shrugged toward the big man as the bartender delivered a highball glass to him and awaited Andy's order. "Everything's settled down, but we needed Ralph here to reestablish peace. And Bret"—she pointed at the red head—"is sore at me because his pushy friend had to be sent out into the cold and not to the warmth of New Orleans where they'd been offering to take me." She bent around Gene to give Bret a big fake smile.

Bartender Ralph scowled. "What'll it be, stranger?"

Andy ordered a draft Bud and reached around Caroline to shake Gene's hand. He gripped firmly, at least, as if he'd found a friend in this place.

Bret stretched out his long arm as well, his hand testing Andy's. "Hey, man, I'm Bret," He was on his way to slurring. "You behave yourself, pardner. And keep an eye on this one." He winked at Caroline, took a seat at the card table, and laughed.

Caroline shook her head, long hair flowing, and the men's heads turned. "The local clientele has a one-track mind. I thought I'd be fine in here with Gene—we *are* together—but boys being boys ..." She pouted.

"Caroline, you *are* the scene, wherever you go." Andy patted her knee. "What in the hell brought you out to the boonies in this weather?" He looked at Gene, who grinned back.

Caroline explained she wanted Gene to "understand" her, and Battle Ground exemplified her Hoosier roots like it did Andy's. Plus the interesting Tippecanoe site lay nearby, though the Indian battlefield was closed. They'd driven around the bare countryside, so unlike California's. And then the snow started so a drink seemed in order. Who could know it would turn into a blizzard? And who would guess such towns had become even less civilized in the five years since she or Andy actually lived in one?

"But now you're here, Andy, so the party can begin." Caroline's blue eyes caught the light. "Let's show Gene how to have a good time on a cold night in a small town." Gene leaned against her shoulder, and Andy wondered how good a time she meant. Caroline always liked her mischief, and they'd enjoyed several three-ways with her girlfriends—he'd considered himself a lucky man. But Gene was another matter. She signaled Ralph for another round.

Andy sipped his beer and scanned the barroom while Caroline and Gene discussed some pretty place in northern California. A surprising number of men were inside; perhaps they hadn't want-ed to be caught at home in the storm. There were exactly three women present besides Caroline, two of them sharing a table with the two best-dressed men in sight: cheap suits, ties loosened at the collars. The third, the waitress, middle-aged, stood at the hulking old Seeburg jukebox, one hand on her thrust-out hip and the oth-er running down the playlist. A country song twanged on about "summer's comin'."

The white walls were dingy with smoke. Subdued voices and secret conversations built into a cloudy din. Two guys threw darts by the restrooms. Blue jeans and flannel shirts, even farmers' overalls, crowded around the one pool table. From the card table, Bret ogled Caroline until one of his buddies nudged him back to their game.

Caroline had told him—in general terms—about her adventures in California. She'd quizzed him about his own vacation there the year before, but he'd stayed in Santa Cruz with friends and remembered San Francisco as a weekend blur of good food and drinking, a strip club he didn't mention. "I'm pretty sure I'll be moving there." She winked at Gene. "Maybe come spring. I don't think I'm cut out for any more of this rube-ery."

Andy blinked. He should have known—she'd called for him on such an awful night as a final act of control. He wanted to punch Gene in his pretty face. And push Caroline down to give her one last good fucking. "Yeah, well, there's plenty of hick to go around. Maybe you'll take some to California with you?"

She slid from her stool to stand in front of Gene and put her hands on his knees. "Will you take me to Cali, darling, away from all this?" Her glance from one to the other made it clear she was including Andy in *this*.

Gene seemed surprised but took her hands and kissed them. "Most certainly." Was he oblivious to Caroline's manipulation?

Andy told them he needed to visit the men's room. He chugged the last of his beer and walked past the jukebox woman—she gave him a good long look as he checked out her nametag, Jamie—and around the cluster of pool players to the raw wooden door marked "Gents." The room stank of piss and cigarettes, their rankness still allowed in bars that kept out children. The true self of the Nite Owl showed here, somehow comforting Andy as it exposed the truth of this night. Wisest to return to the storm, away from Caroline's plotting—retribution, poetic justice, no contrition, no redemption. *He'd* broken up with her, he reminded himself, but that hadn't stopped them from getting together for the occasional benefit of familiar fucking.

Now she'd be gone for good. He washed his hands and dried them on the filthy roller towel retro even in Battle Ground. She wouldn't be able to call him from civilized California to save her sculpted ass.

In the barroom he passed the pool table, nodding at his new compadres who nodded back. The woman choosing music surveyed his hips as Dr. John boogied-up "Goin' Back to New Orleans." Mardi Gras arrived Tuesday. The blizzard made a raucous party in sticky heat sound good. The burly men, minus Bret, dealt poker and the couples proceeded with drinking, both women nudged closer to their dates. But Caroline and Gene weren't at the bar.

The bartender pointed to a table in the front corner. They were talking, fingers flirting on the table to the irritation of Bret, who sat across from Caroline. Fair enough, Andy thought, let Gene take care of her, matters settled. He walked toward them to say goodnight and saw a deck of cards beside Caroline's drink. She shook free of Gene, waved to Andy, stood and pulled the fourth chair out for him.

"Andy, Andy, so far away. What do you love now?" She wrapped herself around him, nuzzling his chest, the smell of her patchouli topping the bar's smoke. She pressed so her breasts massaged him. "How I will miss you." She pulled back and sat, stretching so her sweater showed every curve. She put her elbows on the table and patted the deck. "I thought since we're stuck here we might play some cards. Gene claims he could be a riverboat gambler. And

Bret's willing." She tapped the beer they'd carried over, but Andy remained standing.

Gene simpered, turned into boy by Caroline's spell. "She tells me there's a game in Indiana called 'cutthroat' poker. I'm coming to love this state, hicks or not!"

The locals a couple of empty tables away frowned. "Anytime you don't like the company, you can haul your scrawny ass outta here," Bret bellowed, looking back as if to calm his fellows with his control.

Gene cringed, but his apologetic shrug suggested he didn't understand that Bret would sooner beat him than accept excuses. "Shut up, Gene," Andy said. "This is their place, not ours."

"Hey, okay, guys," Gene muttered. "Sorry."

"And cutthroat is not poker," Caroline said as she shuffled the deck. "It's euchre, three-handed. Andy, don't stick us with teaching Gene that awful game. We need your hand for real poker." She and Andy had last played euchre, boredom-breaker of Indiana towns, with her friend Jessica maybe two years ago. Caroline directed the game into a strip version and debauchery ensued. But unlike Jessica, or Andy, the good-old-boys in this place were wild cards beyond her double-dealing.

Now she seemed nervous, glancing at Bret, not quite meeting his eyes. Andy wondered how long she'd been baiting him, what response to her flirtation got his friend tossed from the bar in a storm.

Bret smiled up at Andy. "C'mon, man. Euchre's not a man's game. We need you for decent poker."

Andy sat and took a drink to mask his irritation. The snow

outside couldn't be worse than Caroline's machinations. He had an impossible urge to smack her, but really should simply leave. Or stay, to witness and enjoy whatever evil she'd deal herself into.

Bret called to his buddies, "Hold my seat, boys. Gonna make a killing over here." The big man ogled Caroline. "I worried we weren't gonna have the chance to get closer, darlin'." He didn't hide his leer. "What'll we be playing' for?"

Caroline raised her brows. "Gene's the guest here. He'll name the game, *darlin'*."

Gene started shuffling. "Four of us? Five card draw or seven card stud. Your choice, Bret." Andy hoped Gene would back his new bravado.

"Oh, stud for us studs, don't ya think?" Bret took a drink then waved his empty glass as Gene offered the cards to Caroline for a cut. "Man, what a night. All that snow, my main man gets tossed for nothing, and now I'm playin' poker with a beautiful girl and other strangers." He tossed in a quarter to set the ante. Expecting a long game, Andy thought. "This town is damn small, but you never know what new joy any given evening will bring through the door." He winked toward Caroline, making sure Andy and Gene understood to what joy he referred.

Andy signaled Ralph his own need for another beer. If not for the cards being dealt his way, he could leave. Nothing horrible awaited Caroline if she'd stay cool. Bret seemed sane and Ralph kept watch. It was only ten, though it felt like 2:00 a.m. in a bad dream. If he didn't leave soon, he might be snowed in with them the entire night.

Jamie the waitress toted over the drinks. "Who's getting this one?" She set down Bret's drink and he didn't move.

"Oh, we'll pay," Caroline said. "We needed the fourth." She smiled sweetly at the older woman.

"No problem, honey." Jamie smacked Bret on his shoulder. "Now Bret, Ralph says you behave yourself." She walked away, her ass sashaying to the music.

They analyzed their cards. Andy showed the queen of spades, the best up card. The spade jack and heart ten were down. With seven cards, a good chance for a straight. Bret showed the deuce of clubs, but with a grin.

Andy bet a quarter and all stayed in. The fourth cards gave Andy the seven of spades, a flush conceivable. Gene fiddled with his change on the table when he paired with the ten of clubs, dangerous. Caroline played with her hair. Bret's grin morphed into a poker face with another two. "California Girls" came on the jukebox. Andy checked to confirm who'd made the choice and Jamie winked.

Gene dealt the fifth cards. Bret's ace of clubs seemed little help except as a kicker. Andy couldn't resist smiling at his nine of spades, but threes spades showing would make the others nervous. Caroline's club queen drew Gene's optimistic comment "possible straight" before he dealt himself the ace of diamonds. "My tens still bet." Another quarter lead, but Bret scratched the back of his neck then pushed out a quarter raise. "Fifty cents to you, Mr. Spades."

Andy restrained from bumping. Caroline and Gene stayed in, too. Raises at these rates wouldn't drive out a homeless bum, but each of them reckoned the others' body language. Andy focused on Bret and scratched his chin.

The sixth cards came out: the heart four for Bret, seven of hearts to Andy, heart jack Caroline—this time Gene didn't mention the more likely straight—and heart three to Gene. "All hearts, that's us." Bret laughed.

Gene nodded. "Tens check."

He was trying to pick up information, so why not mislead. "My sevens'll bet a buck." He let the bill float into the pot.

Caroline winked, signaling Andy's game. He wanted to shout "shut up" but the damage was done. Bret said, "See your buck, big talker, and raise another." He wasn't raising with a pair of deuces; he probably held three of them.

Caroline stayed, and stayed quiet. Andy knew her game, too, poker at least. She might well be one card off the open straight, as he was. Gene stayed too, but Andy's heart ten made it unlikely Gene had the other. The pot was good, considering where it started. Bret sipped his drink and continued to eye Caroline, now more approving than lustful. Andy wanted to slap one of them, or both. Gene looked oblivious, so a slap for him, too.

"Final cards down, gentlemen," Gene announced. "And lady." How nice if Gene forgot Caroline, went back to San Francisco. Left her here where she and Andy belonged.

Bret could head to New Orleans or wherever, though only he belonged here in Battleground. He lifted his three hold cards then counted his money on the table, sure sign a bluff would follow. Andy edged up the eight of diamonds, his straight made, queen high. He'd rather have hit the flush, but good enough. Caroline held her last card high. She eyed Bret as if to signal, you take him out.

Gene's tens were still betting, but he shrugged. Bret tossed in a dollar and Andy raised one and Caroline bumped with another. Gene folded. Bret hesitated, checked Caroline for clues and matched the raises. Andy could simply match the bets and collect the decent winnings. They'd more than pay for Bret's drink. And maybe chase him from the table.

Caroline smiled in a way Andy recognized and hated, the merciless sneer she'd given when she and Jessica sent him away so they could spend the rest of the night together without him. The vengeful look as she told him how much he'd regret breaking up with her, before she sashayed away.

She turned her cards to show a ten and the heart ace for the straight. The bitch. She pulled the cash toward her, leaving a quarter for the next ante.

Bret smirked. "You didn't see that comin', man? Hell, I just stayed to pad the pot for the little lady." He showed matched the two deuces with paired aces.

Andy didn't show his cards. Let them guess, as if they needed to. Cocky people like Caroline—and Bret—loved to be on the winning end. He hoped the next round would show how well they handled losing.

But the second hand played quickly. Andy dropped on the fourth card at Bret's raise. Caroline stayed in long enough to sucker more cash from Gene before Bret won with three nines.

Bret finished his drink and looked to his buddies still playing hard and loud. "Cleanin' up, fellas!" He waved for Jamie. "Let me get this one, my new friends."

What crap. *Noblesse oblige* from this horny yokel.

"We'd wipe out the house in New Orleans, honey. Hope you're still thinkin' 'bout goin'." Bret wasn't playing for the money—he wanted to get all over Caroline.

"Oh, Bret, you are quite the player." She flicked her hair.

"Boys of Summer" came on the jukebox and Gene headed for the men's room. Andy left Caroline and Bret to their flirtation and stepped outside to check the weather. The calm wind stalled the few heavy flakes of snow. Maybe they'd forget about the game so he could say goodbye. Parked cars across Railroad Street appeared a chain of igloos, but the street had been plowed. He'd be able to clear his car and leave. The bar's parking lot to the north fared even better—lanes plowed so piles of gray snow castled the entry. Ten inches or so were drifting, good most winters for second or third place in central Indiana standings.

Inside at the bar, Andy watched the TV with Jamie. "Breaking news" covered salt trucks careening out to attack the city's streets and county roads. A guy at the bar complained that if the storm waited a day, they'd've gotten off work on Monday. Ralph said it would be two days before things got back to normal in Battle Ground. Jamie told him, "You get outta here before that, sweetheart."

Andy saw Gene thread his way around the pool players, a couple of whom glared at his designer jeans. Andy paid for his beer and returned to the table. Bret and Caroline were leaning in so their heads met. When he and Gene sat, the two lovebirds tilted back. Caroline said, "Me and Bret think we should all pack up outta here and go to New Orleans."

Gene let out a worried snicker. Bret's smile changed from lecherous to corrupt. "It's not snowing there, it's nearly Mardi Gras, and I got a standing invite from old friends. Those yahoos won't go." He nodded at his former poker buddies. "New Orleans's too classy for them. Andy, you could take a couple of days off work, couldn't you?"

Caroline probed Andy, close-mouthed. She was serious, or something close to it, and Andy wanted to kill her. Bret seemed pretty good-humored, but every man set toying limits, and Caroline didn't know Bret's. Andy noted the big man rolling the fingers of one hand on the table in a drumbeat, while the other angled his highball to measure its emptiness. "I can be packed in five minutes, we drive to Lafayette in my big ol' Tribeca to pack your stuff, and we're in the Big Easy by tomorrow lunch."

Andy figured Bret worked at Subaru, made a bunch more money than he did clerking at the university library. If Bret was union he could wrangle time off more or less as he liked. Where had Andy's degree gotten him? Stuck in a state with no jobs for humanists, in this godforsaken bar with a bitch and a bagful of frustrations.

Gene twitched in his seat. "But, Caroline, I'm here to see Indiana." Bret gave him a scowl.

"Have you ever been to New Orleans, Eugene?" She tilted her head so her hair cascaded. "Mardi Gras? Lots better than days sitting inside." She turned to Andy. "And I'd have all my boys around to steer me out of trouble."

Bret beamed. "That's the truth. I can tell from our little game here we'll all get along fine." He slapped the table. "Now you don't want your sweet girl traveling all that way alone with a brute like me." He rose and stretched, half-covered a belch, and sized up Andy. "Or do you?" He headed toward the restrooms and disappeared into the pool table crowd.

Andy scowled at Caroline. "Are you plain crazy? Bret isn't a fucking pussycat." He grabbed her hand. "He thinks you're fucking serious."

Caroline leaned back, her sweater pulling tight. "Who's to say I'm not?" She planted her elbows on the table. "I hate this cold. I hate this state." She appraised the room then settled on Andy. "And I don't care much for current company." Her nostrils flared. "Isn't one of you going to take me away from here?"

Her pale skin reddened. Drunk, Caroline could play pathetic. She struggled to her feet and Gene tried to restrain her, but she pulled away and headed toward the restrooms.

Bret appeared among the pool players and reached after Caroline with a huge arm, but she dodged into the ladies room. Bret stopped at the big chrome Seeburg, ran his finger on the playlist. He clenched and relaxed his shoulders and twisted his thick neck as if straightening out a crick.

Gene asked what they should do and Andy snapped, "What would you like to do, Gene? Have me decide which one of you to kill first?"

Caroline shooed Bret away from the jukebox toward their table. She balanced, her nose pressed against the machine's glass, to focus on possible choices.

Bret arrived at the table smiling as if they'd all become old friends, and Gene headed toward Caroline. The pool players gravitated around the table's far end and checked out Caroline's posture, her ass high and tight and, whether she intended it or not, aimed right toward them. Gene attempted to straighten her up, but she pushed quarters into the slot. Gene glanced at Andy, shrugged, and entered the restroom. Time to leave.

But Bret laid his arm around Andy's shoulder. "Man, let's hit the road. She won't go without you, and I'm not joking, we made a connection." He breathed alcohol into Andy's ear. "I'll get you a chick in New Orleans. Even someone for that pansy." His grip tightened. "Hell, man, it's Mardi Gras." He sounded like a whiny kid except for the muscular arm.

Andy straightened so his body displayed its own lithe strength. He motioned Bret to sit then placed his hands on the chair's arms, trapping him. "Man, don't try this tonight." He backed off at Bret's glare. "With Caroline you just have to be patient. Ask her out, fine. Take her to dinner. Let her see you'll take care of her."

Bret seemed to sober and Andy pushed on. "That's what she's really after. A man's got to come off more solid than tough."

Bret inhaled, chest expanding. Andy winked. "But in some ways she's worth it."

Andy stepped back and Bret sprawled out, workboots stretching into the room. "Seems so," Bret said, watching Caroline as she headed toward them, strides again confident when the Animals' sultry version of "House of the Rising Sun" began to play.

Bret held Caroline's chair, eyes on Andy. She took her time settling into the seat. "Let's play poker, pardners." She pointed pistol fingers at Andy and Gene, who sat, confused.

Andy sensed he'd gone all in now, unless or until he got her out of the Nite Owl. Caroline and Bret kicked Andy and Gene's asses, trading deals, passing looks, and collecting cash for the next three hands. The conversation meandered through the joys of New Orleans—Cajun food, beignets, raised graves, mansions, mimosas, Spanish moss. Only Bret had been to Mardi Gras—his friends there were real—but he played shy about the excesses. "Booze, beads, and bare … well, you know." Caroline winked at Andy. To think he'd once believed he loved her. He tried to concentrate on the moment. What did he still want from her?

Caroline lost interest in the game and stood to stretch. Bret counted his money and asked who wanted a cigar. Gene slurred, "I'm in." He seemed relieved things turned out so friendly. Andy agreed to try one, too.

Caroline scanned the table. "And one for me, too, Bret darlin'." She used a dancehall floozy voice. "Andy, you go pick a couple more songs. We should hit the road after."

Andy located opportune music while Ralph appeared to quiz Bret as he set the humidor on the bar. Bret chose cigars, then waved Andy over to help carry drinks for them all. "Jamie's left us for the night, folks. No need to tip." He passed Caroline's drink. "Around here, winners buy. Just good manners."

Bret displayed three thick coronas and one slimmer stick. Caroline grabbed the panatela. "Mine, I presume." She ran her fingers along the brown stalk, sniffing and turning up her pert nose. Andy realized that with Jamie clocked out, all the good girls had gone home. She licked the cigar's tip. "Haven't smoked one of these in years."

Andy lit a fat cigar and coughed. Bret lit Caroline's, his hands tenting hers to protect the fire. Andy grimaced. Bad vibes kept fighting to the surface here in Battle Ground, or maybe they were merely his disordered feelings for Caroline in retreat.

Bret made them stand for a toast, flaring cigars hazing smoke over the table. Caroline nuzzled Bret, who beamed like a red-combed rooster. Gene's tan paled at first puff, a ghost found haunting the wrong house. Andy said he needed fresh air.

The snow had stopped and Railroad Street looked mostly cleared. The winding state highway to Lafayette would be fine. He imagined speeding around its curves to test the ice, but only his feet skidded on the sidewalk. He tossed the cigar into a plowed pile of gray-stained snow. Fuck Bret if he thought his rank gift wasted.

Gene sat at the table playing solitaire, bewildered.

Andy checked the cards. "Four of spades plays there, Gene. Where'd they go?"

Gene pointed over his shoulder. Bret leaned on the juke box. The Pointer Sisters' "Lady Marmalade," Andy's choice, blasted out its none-too-subtle French, "*Voulez-vous coucher* … ." Andy laughed at the big man's foolishness—Caroline had him lassoed. One of the pool players slapped Bret on the back.

Caroline came out of the women's room, riled or just drunk, and checked the action. She smirked toward Andy and waved Bret to her. They disappeared into a corner behind the table. Now she'd play the trump card, deliver the *coup de grâce*. He put on his coat and signaled Gene to do the same. He hoped Bret would still be laughing.

They went to the bar and settled their bill. Gene insisted on providing the lion's share though he'd lost more than Andy. Only fair, Andy thought. "You might want to warm up her car." Andy patted Caroline's purse which Gene held awkwardly. "Keys in the right-side pocket."

Gene flinched as if he'd forgotten it was a cold snowy night in Indiana. "Oh, yeah, I guess the princess will desire her carriage heated." He sniffed. "Good to meet you, Andy. Caroline does go on."

Andy gestured a-okay. "See ya around, Gene. She'll be out in a minute. Good luck." Gene pushed open the door with his shoulder, smoke trailing after him.

Andy turned to the barroom but Caroline was not hastening toward him as he hoped. He drained his beer and waved Ralph off another. He took a deep breath and stepped toward the back of the room, his thighs tightening, forearms flexing by instinct.

Behind the remaining pool players Bret pressed Caroline against the wall, her face twisted away from his kiss or threat. No doubt she'd provoked it, but Bret's posture, shoulders bent around her and hips angled in, came from expectation beyond frustration. Andy picked up his strides and tested his fists, then blindsided Bret with a shove, sending the big man against the men's room's door, shocked red with anger.

"Get the hell out of here, Caroline." She froze.

Now!" She stepped from the wall, shaking. "Gene's got your car. Go!"

Bret straightened and snarled when Caroline rushed away across the barroom. "You bitch," Bret yelled and the pool players formed a line to the side. Andy watched her grab her coat and push the door open without putting it on.

Then Bret was on him.

His red stubble scratched Andy's cheek as he missed a head-butt, but lurched against the table as Andy moved, arms crossed chest-high in defense. Andy spun past the pool players. Bret lumbered after him.

At the end of the bar, Bret grabbed Andy's shoulder, pressed him against the bar rail. "You!" He drew back his right arm and Andy braced as best he could, his arms up again, but he knew what was coming.

Ralph's voice boomed, "Bret!" and a baseball bat pushed Bret's swing against his chest. Ralph stepped between them, his bulk a barricade against Bret's shoving. "Get the hell out of here, kid," Ralph bellowed. "And don't you or your friends come again."

Andy pulled on his coat. "Not ever," Ralph commanded. Andy brushed himself off while Bret gulped air as Ralph settled him onto a bar stool. At the door, Andy glanced back and Bret stood shaking his fist, shouting, "You! You!"

Snow blew around him and Caroline's car swept by on Railroad Street, no horn blast of farewell or cheer for his survival. Andy trudged backward into the street, tracking the bar's door. "Nite" "Owl" "Inn" blinked on in blue, but he saw the words accusing "You You You."

SCOUTS

THE TWO BOYS—YOUNG MEN—EXPECTED TO do more masculine things camping in the national forest south of the Grand Canyon. Scout up kindling, dig a fire pit, haul water from a stream, fight off the mountain cold with the bottle of Jack they'd bought using their fake IDs that morning in Vegas. Instead, the campground provided a low grill, firewood, a communal tap beside the shower house. The August evening stayed warm as heat from the nearby desert rose as the sun set.

They cooked hot dogs and beans and swigged the bourbon while they argued over how to deal with any confrontational bear and mused about the bent-tree lean-to they'd built in camp when their friendship was still in its boyhood. They laughed remembering how their friend Ryan had startled and peed himself when a fellow scout shook a catalpa pod by his pup-tent's flap and cried "snake!" They admitted it been cruel but decided they should be forgiven. Ryan had eventually laughed, too. They'd merely been boys being boys.

The sun completed its descent as they finished dinner. Their campsite stood separated from the others by tall pines and scrub. Some chatter drifted in, broken by laughter. They went silent as if to will their neighbors to quiet down. Then one walked to the shelter for more water they'd heat on the fire to do the dishes. The other policed the fireside mess, tossed the bun wrapper onto the embers, watched it shrivel.

They discussed the route to conclude the grand tour of the West their parents had financed as graduation presents. They'd hike some more of the Canyon's rim tomorrow then drive through Flagstaff to the Petrified Forest and overnight in a motel at Canyon de Chelly on the Navajo Reservation. The next night they'd camp at Mesa Verde before speeding south to I-40 for the eastward haul.

But first this forest's beauty. Had native scouts camped here, considered the Canyon beautiful, or merely an obstacle? The other campers' noise wore away. When a dry gust rattled the brush they held their breath in the stasis, hoping a deer, anything animal, had been drawn to the dying fire. But nothing came.

They looked into the sky as if an eagle might descend. Stars twinkled by the thousands like strewn glitter, so many because they were a mile high and far away from cities, they concluded, awed for the hazy half-hour it took to smoke a joint.

Then an owl's call reassured that they had indeed entered a place more wild than the Midwestern homes they would soon be leaving, in different directions, forever. They looked at each other, appreciating for perhaps the first time the togetherness in such aloneness.

In the tent, they lay very still, listening only to the other's breathing. One stirred and reached out a hand. The other returned the warm, tender, urgent touch.

TOYLAND

1969

I'M PICKING HER UP AT HER PARENTS' house out in the snowy farmland, knowing I will get laid, my first time. Knock on the door and kid brother answers, looks up at me through the storm glass. He gives me a twisted little smile and nods me inside where a TV's singing out the welcome medley to *The Wonderful World of Disney*. Sunday night, seven-thirty.

"Terry's upstairs getting ready," her mother says as she hangs my heavy jacket on a coat rack. "You met her at Marcia's party, Joe? Did you have a nice Christmas? Go sit down. Root beer or lemonade?" she says, then heads off down a hallway and my nerves settle.

Their Christmas tree glows in the otherwise dark dining room. In the living room, the father in his big stuffed recliner nods at me with a tight smile. I sit on the end of the couch away from the kid. Dad leans forward and holds out a bowl. "Popcorn?" he asks. "We're going to watch Disney." Tinker Bell makes the fireworks explode on the TV screen over the Magic Kingdom's turreted castle.

No defenses here, just the isolated comfort of farm living. He's wearing a plaid flannel shirt and a brown wool vest, those slippers with the furry lining. Does he know his daughter is easy? His furrowed face holds seeds of country wisdom, not worldly knowledge.

An ad comes on the TV with cartoon ballerinas and the little boy bounces the couch then reaches for a handful of popcorn. He nods at me, tries to connect. "You like *my sister*?" he asks. "Girls—yuck!" Was I ever like him—wanting to be the center of everyone's attention?

"Be polite, Brian," his father says, speaking around me. "Your sister is popular." He smiles. "You're the oddball, buddy."

I wait for him to say something like, 'you'll like girls soon enough'—the kid's eight or nine—but no such male bonding is forthcoming. Dad bends his small mouth in apology, but there's a kind of sizing me up. Has he reminded himself what 'popular' might really mean? Did guys like this ever get any before they got married? I know lots of farm boys and they're plenty ready to stud.

The kid glares at me as if I'm to blame for him getting the lecture. He chomps down more popcorn and slurps his root beer. Mother brings a pitcher of lemonade, pours a glass for me, fills the dad's, leaves again. A summer drink in winter, I think, anxious to get to the booze, Southern Comfort at Terry's request. Rounded it up from a friend's older brother who's loaning me his apartment. He gave me some tips on Terry—"kiss her neck, man, and all will be yours." Does the mother, flowing around in her slippers, her round hips rolling beneath her house dress, have a sweet spot, too?

Dad catches me following her movements but seems almost flattered as he watches her himself. They have two other kids, a boy and a girl both in college like me, but I'm an only child. Terry's a high school senior. The boy must be an afterthought.

The Disney episode comes back on and I settle back, wondering what's keeping Terry so long. I sip the tart lemonade. It's *Babes in Toyland*, a movie I was too old for even when it came out years ago, despite Annette Funicello with her fantasy breasts in the major role as Mary Quite Contrary. Says the kid, "We watched the first part last week. It's pretty weird." He looks at me as if we might become friends, squirms on the couch and shakes his head in dramatic yeses.

I hear footsteps gallop on the stairs, and father chuckles just as Terry pops into the room. Is he laughing at the goofy costumes on the screen—and sheep!—or Terry's joyful entrance? She likes attention, a girl just this side of cute and a few pounds overweight, but the plumpness improves her chest, and that I know I like. She's got a funny kind of mouth, small with uneven lips always a little twisted. I hear she does nice things with it, but will I know if it's really good? First time for that, too. I feel about as green as the kid.

The smile and wink she gives me should surely signal trouble to dad, but what could he do about it anyway? So he focuses on the TV, pointing out classic fairy tale references the kid may have forgotten. It occurs to me that TV has replaced fairy tales. I think that's a pretty smart thought, my brains hopefully one of the reasons Terry's happy to please me. That plus of course I'm good-looking in a budding, long-haired hippie kind of way, a disturbing quality to fathers, including my own who lets me know it. Plus I went to high school one town over, surely making me a suspect stranger. But her dad doesn't seem to care. Terry sits down next to me and leans her shoulder against mine. "Daddy, Joe goes to Purdue," she says, almost cooing. "He's friends with Marcia Bowman, so he comes highly recommended." Marcia's a girl from a neighboring family whose brother knew what I needed.

She taps her father's slippered foot to get at least part of his attention, but he just says, "I know, I know, now watch the show." He looks at us and remembers it's a date. "You're welcome to watch with us. Stay out of this awful weather," he says flatly.

It is cold, but it's barely snowing. If I said, 'oh, can we please, I just love watching Disney,' he'd keel over in shock. Annette is crooning moon-eyed with Tommy Sands, her breasts made modest—but even more tempting— by a Technicolor-blue milkmaid's dress.

Terry nudges my leg and kid brother watches her as he reaches for some more popcorn. Little spy. Probably got his sneakiness from one of those Disney dramas where kids are detectives. "Are you gonna kiss her?" he blurts out and Terry's face reddens.

"Brian, you brat!" she screams. She slaps at his hand and popcorn goes flying. "You little shit!" He howls and then giggles as he folds fetal into the couch's corner.

Dad springs up in the recliner so fast I think it may launch him into space. "You two, behave! Brian, clean that up!" He stands and glances sternly at Terry. "And you, young lady, watch your mouth." He shakes his head and looks at me with a kind of exasperation I can't place. "Are you going out, or what?" he asks, looking at both of us.

She smiles up at him and tells two fibs. "Daddy, we'd love to stay but there's a party at Lisa's and they're expecting us." She stands and wags her hand behind her round ass so I'll take it, the hand that is. Dad settles back into *Toyland* as we walk to the foyer. He doesn't say good-bye and I hope I haven't pissed him off, but I'm glad that, even though I bet he doesn't drink, he's not my father.

Little Brian is down on his knees picking up popcorn, staring at us. Dad asks him, "What'd I miss?" But the kid just sniggles. Dad doesn't like being ignored and says, "You, get upstairs," and the kid runs past us, glaring. Mom shows up, shaking her head, helps Terry and me into our winter jackets, straightening my collar like my own mother would. She looks me in the eyes, kind of sad, I think. Then Terry grabs my gloved hand and says, "We gotta go, Mom. Don't wait up," as we swing out the door onto the snow-patched porch. The cold feels good to me.

We trudge to my car and I open the door for her and she smiles as she climbs into the low seat, nervous maybe, or ready. I wonder why she's like this, so easy. I want to like her though I was only introduced to her at the party a few days ago. I hope I'll like what we're going to do. I open my own door, relieved to have made it out of their house, its rituals. I'm undamaged except for Annette and Tommy singing in my head. Who could have expected Disney and lemonade, for Christ's sake?

I start up the engine and its rev promises warming. Terry says, "You look so good, good enough to eat." She touches my thigh just where the jacket ends. "They drive me crazy. Especially that little ass Brian. But at least the others weren't there. They're home from school but they can get out of that house any time they want."

I wait for the engine to steady and the heat to even. The house is a puzzle of lights in the dark night—living room and its flickering TV, the dining room aglow with Christmas. Upstairs a light comes on in a window as Terry's fingers tighten on my leg and she bends into me. "Kiss me," she says. "You have to kiss me lots." And so I do, soft lips, and my hands finding other softness as she sighs with happiness. "God, I want you," she says. "I wanted to do it right there with the TV blaring. Right there in front of them." Her tongue is all over my teeth and her hand rubs my crotch, and I feel her farm girl strength.

"Hey, hey now," I say, and pull back. When she pouts at my resistance, I kiss her gently, trying to be kind or something. "Let's get out of here."

She slides a bit to the right and I fiddle with the shift. I turn on my lights and look forward to gauge the best route out, my tire tracks still visible in the snow.

Terry turns on the radio and rushes through stations so the music flashes from rock to carols, until she finds a romantic crooner's tune like our fathers might have dug at our age, Frank Sinatra maybe, to drive *Toyland*'s sugar plums from our heads.

I turn the wheel as we start to roll, and scan the place we're leaving. It's easy for me to make out the boy's face pressed against the icy glass in the upstairs window. I imagine his little mouth puckered into a taunting kiss, his eyes wide open as they follow us into the darkness.

MID-LIVES

JONAH LOUNGES IN A CHAISE ON THE deck, looks up from the novel he's reading, James Salter's masterpiece of ambivalence, *All That Is*, sees a cloud in the sky shaped like ... a rabbit, no doubt projecting the neighborhood bunny he's watched munch grass in the alley. Salter might approve of Jonah's distraction—the novel wanders character to character, place to place. Does Jonah's own life meander, half-begun, half-over, will vs. fate not war but a perpetual draw? It's almost enough to drive him back to the piano where his own composition, a neo-romantic trio, dawdles half-finished. He can return anytime to his art, if not life's passion.

Jonah questions whether he should have traveled again to Poland with his wife Anna, working on her post-minimalist constructions (Richard Tuttle her hero) at a retreat in Krakow, a lovely city now embracing western ways—shopping malls, multiplexes, hamburger joints. Anna reports by email that a new Cinnabon graces the main square. So the change, Jonah responded flippantly, is not all for the worse.

But in fact Anna is this evening heading by tram for the house of the artist Bronisław Kosmatka with whom she's flirted for years, again yesterday when he lectured at the retreat. Public transportation remains excellent in Eastern Europe though autos are taking over the narrow streets. Anna wonders if Bronek will make a move tonight, or if she need be bolder. She has shed her bra, glad for her still sturdy body. Though there are younger women at whom to ogle, men still leer in the gym.

Jonah listens as a young woman's singing drifts from the north, wannabe Joplin or Winehouse. An art fair has tightened local traffic all weekend. As distracting as a lawnmower, or Cleo, their cat who, disappointed at Anna's absence, will not stop mewing. Jonah has closed the patio screen, but the kitty's shriek breaks out. Or is Cleo joining the singer's wailing?

Jonah considers calling the earthy Maggie, who has signaled she is available. He understands that Maggie craves Anna more, but the ménage Jonah dreams of hasn't sparked, Anna unnecessarily concerned about aging. She remains entirely attractive—body and mind and artist's heart. No wonder Maggie, a younger impoverished painter, desires her.

All morning Maggie has prepared for a visit from Cheryl, her suburban lover, a luncheon salad the excuse invoked each trysting. Cheryl refuses to end her bad marriage, needing the money and connections she'd lose cutting out on her own. Same old story, Maggie bemoans. I'm good enough for sex but not for love. She gazes out her walk-up's dusty window as cars speed by below. Would an affair with Anna and Jonah be different, those two already in love? Only once did they all come close, hugging in parking lot shadows after a symphony concert. Anna will never call, yet Jonah's tempting talk continues. In his car, they have brought each other pleasure, invoking the taste of Anna. Maggie wishes Cheryl would arrive early, but still an hour to wait, touching no one. Does she bring this third-wheel status on herself?

Imagining the three-way himself, Jonah resists going inside where only the cat and guilty laziness await. He could visit the fair, check out the plaintive singer, much younger than himself, a redhead, he imagines, delusionally seeking a career in music like many of his students. Last semester, inflated grading made him culpable of both creating false hopes and abetting standards' free-fall. But what excuse for his own mind, darting between the fair and Krakow, to Maggie's bedroom which he's only imagined. He calculates potential gains or losses, the crisis of desire lost in the stasis between will and fate. Jonah follows the cloud as it becomes a puff of smoke. He feels as if his very spirit has departed … or wants to.

Anna debarks the tram but no one meets her. Bronisław, a sculptor, is sometimes overinvolved in his work. Marble, his current expensive medium, demands special concentration. One small slip of the chisel and … *kaput*. Though they have met privately only twice before, three years ago his huge hands held her to him, rough fingers budged her nipples, salty tongue made promises she hopes he now will keep—*if* she has retained her appeal. She can't judge by Jonah, who seems excited only by deviance, silks tying her, a riding crop stinging her ass, a plea to enjoy Maggie together. *His* fantasy flirtation, though she hasn't discouraged him. Maggie *is* desirable. If passion showed first between just the two women, perhaps … She feels no guilt regarding Bronek, only apprehension of rejection. As Jonah reminds her, she has earned more confidence in herself. She walks down the linden-lined street as globed lamps come on, gilding the leaves and pavement wet from an afternoon shower. Only two blocks to his studio.

Jonah notes that the clouds have disappeared, the emptiness making the sky bluer, more vast. Sirens sound south, but nothing here is burning, not even the younger neighbors' fire pit, which he has considered extinguishing, sledgehammer to smoky bricks. He puts aside Salter's circuitous story, goes inside, feeds the cat, taps a single note on the piano. As he showers, Jonah remembers a girlfriend who knelt beneath him there. Something to ask of Anna? He intends no humiliation, only a spark of younger days, when the smallest emotional bump had meaning. He towels himself dry, picturing Anna astride Maggie, not the other way around.

Anna knocks a few times before Bronek shoulders open the heavy door, leering beneath sweaty brow and mussed hair. Tarps carpet the concrete floor of the Soviet-era building. Under floodlights a tall block of marble with pinkish veins seems to express a woman unveiling from tunic, exposing curves. Anna looks around for a model, but only Bronek is present, directing her around the piece. "It means to represent all women," he explains, a commission for a young man who has made killing on the internet. He poses Anna next to it. "Yes, all women." He guides her hand over the cold contours then pulls her to him. "Are you ready?"

Of course, she whispers, she has never felt more desired. She kneels, provoking his commands.

Maggie tries to hold Cheryl at her door, but the older woman pulls way. From now on they must be "just friends," Cheryl insisted when, after only lunch, Maggie lifted a fingertip of flan toward her lips. Cheryl claims to be reconciling with her husband, but does her look challenge Maggie to fight for their connection? Instead she weakens under Cheryl's gaze, can invent no compromise, tears up. Cheryl walks to the staircase and down, not once looking back up from her creaky footfalls.

Walking through the sunny fair, Jonah assesses pot-throwers, garden-variety metalsmiths, photographers testing the limits of motion blurring. They sit in tall chairs under canvas awnings, explain their art to passersby. They'll be well burned by the season's end, perhaps with enough cash to fund next year's journeys in increasingly decrepit vans. Jonah attends one such event a year, not for the "art," but to confirm the wisdom of his choice to teach, its stability. He can still create, invoke the music's notes. He'll earn more from his two commissions this year these gated nomads gross.

He notices the youthfulness of most people he passes. At a stage by the river, the singer he heard earlier continues as evening falls. Jonah follows as she moves on tiptoes straining for too high a note. She does have red hair, dyed highlights. He recognizes other bands on the billboard from the local ad-rag—Terrible Twos (featuring two sets of twins), Nutcrackers Sweet (all girls), Fiery Brimstone. The crowd has reduced to gawkers finishing beers, listening to "Carolyna Cruel," a brand meant to tough-up the girl's soft features, as intend her many tattoos. He realizes he knows her, his student some years back, Carolyne, with a "y." Her voice was never strong enough to aspire professionally, but her work ethic was exemplary. Her eyes widen as Jonah nears the stage.

Jonah stops twenty feet away as she finishes the song. He applauds with a dozen others, her fellow performers or wayward drunks. "Ta-da," she screams, making the microphone blare, then runs from the stage toward him. "Professor, I can't believe you're here. How'd you like it?"

"Stunning." Jonah offers a handshake to which she responds with a moist hug. His false praise seems a necessary evil. She lets his hands slide over her hips, her eyes fluttering.

Anna steps from under Bronisław's umbrella, onto the tram. She presses her cheek to the cold window and waves goodbye even as he hulks into the shadows. She feels not a loss but a hope exchanged for some new, hazy purpose. Under his weight she felt joined to the lustrous marble, a shimmering sea, a sunburst horizon. Where to now? Back to her tiny Krakow apartment, then cooped in the airplane, then home where Jonah will hold her, lightly as ever, though she knows that she is bound.

On Jonah's vine-camouflaged deck, smoke and chatter drift from the neighbors. The girl—Carolyne, he reminds himself—struggles to stand, her lipstick messed from their contortions. As he'd groped and kissed her, she whispered, "I always wanted this," then threw herself onto him, exuberant as her songs. Now Jonah rolls over on the chaise, raises a finger to trace the rose tattoo on her thigh as she pulls on her clothes. He asks her to stay. She seems to wonder where she is, who he is. Regrets. Youth as always, Jonah thinks, never satisfied—false hopes, bad paths, remorse ... until life's inevitable ambiguity resets to realistic standards.

She stands at the steps. "Thanks ... I guess, but no." And he needn't drive her home. She walks down the alley, cell phone to ear, and Jonah looks above her to the stars hazy in the city's glow, moon obscured by clouds. A night meant for walking, the longer, slower, route the better.

Inside, Jonah foregoes his email and so doesn't read that Anna is happy to be returning early, day after tomorrow. He realizes he has left Salter's novel half-finished under the chaise where it will absorb the morning dew. Intention or destiny, he leaves it be. At the piano he nods at the lined paper, his scrawled notes. He is in the middle of the piece, the middle of life, the middle of women, he thinks, not just beginning or already lost. He hits a note, stands listening to its echoes.

———◆———

SEX ADDICT

A MID THE CONFUSION OF HUNGRY MOURNERS WHO'D invaded her father's house, Liz watched her husband Ben help the pretty girl gather a plate of finger sandwiches, salads, and chips. If a funeral didn't stop him, what would? Take some shrimp, too, Ben urged, his words clear to Liz even across the room. What was her name, daughter of her sister-in-law Charlene's second husband? Jenna. Liz had stopped by her college graduation party a year ago.

Ben held the girl's arm directing her to the split-level living room, one of his fantastic stories no doubt spinning. Liz turned away into the jalousied porch, wishing a deer might grace the backyard, her father's spirit somehow returning to check up on her. At the end of summers, deer habitually gleaned the garden's leftovers. They'd been raiding the property so long her father claimed they'd lost all fear.

No fear either among the family as they traded stories about her dad and congratulated one another on recent successes. Even Ben's gay brother and cynical sister received approval though they had stayed in Georgia. Their mother Margaret had flown up to brag on her brood, treating Ben like he was still an Eagle Scout.

Liz's mother-in-law had the solid build of a wrestler and the southern accent of a belle. She was updating a second cousin on Ben's flying career—Navy Top Gun, United, now private jets for his boss, a big shot tech inventor, as if the boss's genius attached to Ben. She failed to mention Ben's exciting run-ins with jealous husbands, angry fathers, and the occasional pimp. Her mother-in-law knew all about Ben's addiction and that Liz balanced its costs in the household's ledger. What other wife calmly budgeted for STD tests? At least with Margaret around, Liz needn't be the one to defend him though his problem was such old news that was rarely needed.

Margaret seemed also interested in items of greater value. She casually asked Liz what a mid-century modern house on three wooded acres in gated Dune Acres on the Lake Michigan shore was worth these days.

Liz sighed. "Oh, we'll worry about that later, Margaret." For now she intended to hold onto her dad's house. No need for Margaret to know the property was worth at least a million, though Ben must realize its value.

Like the estate, the family had become complicated, her brother Mark dead ten years now and her sister Lynette so uninterested she hadn't even flown in for the funeral from the yoga retreat she owned in Bali. And with her father buried, this house now emptied of its real life. Her prayers that her nuclear family find peace—their two boys civil if not loving, and Ben satisfied sexually with Liz—had gone unanswered. He was an addict. It was a sickness. He deserved forgiveness, but she found little left to give.

But Margaret, widening her smile, would provide plenty. "Oh, goodie, Ben does so love this place."

In the kitchen Liz circled the table, pretending to want more. She glanced into the living room where Ben's chatter held Jenna rapt. Liz imagined the girl's thighs warming, her mind losing logic. She'd been there herself, all those years ago. He knew how to pick 'em.

Charmer. Sweet talker. Thief of hearts. Ben played the attractive older man like a pro—attentive to women, well-heeled, welcome anywhere. Her senior year, over her dad's warnings, Liz fell hard for the handsome and well-liked pilot-in-training. And, true, the sex was great and lots of it. Even as Ben's problem showed, her father encouraged her to stick with the marriage. Forgiveness was divine and Ben became her father's favorite through his cheerful help with the house and garden and with steadying Liz. She'd made it for twenty-five years and their second son just graduated college with honors. She hoped her father wasn't watching from heaven as Ben patted the young woman's knee.

Even for Ben the seduction seemed bold. The girl's giggles supplanted what would more aptly be screams. Liz cringed. He knew no restraints. With their boys out of the house, divorcing him became plausible. But he'd chosen her well. On the day she buried her father, how could she imagine herself also without Ben?

Someone nudged up beside her and Liz smelled her sister-in-law Charlene's perfume, too sweet for her matronly body. Since Liz's big brother Mark had died—quick T-cell leukemia—Charlene had gone to pot, the cooking pot that is. Somehow she'd attracted a new husband before getting so big, and now the little man stood beside her, his head bobbing. Both looked stern and

Charlene glanced to the living room as if to ask, what is going on with your husband and my stepdaughter? Liz had heard that the girl was no angel herself.

But most of the family accepted the reality of Ben's problem as disease, not promiscuity. On such a large extended quilt, many squares bore red letters for a host of sins. As bad to have a drunkard falling over tables. Liz smiled grimly at Charlene—please understand—but earned only a twisted smile in return. Liz packed a plate with desserts and floated toward the living room. If Charlene wanted the dalliance broken up, she'd have to do it herself.

Liz stopped on the last step and Ben's hand rose from Jenna's knee in a subtle wave and the girl blushed. He gave her knee a father-like pat and stood. She saw his erection soften as he rose. His peck to Liz's cheek implied more sister than wife, though the one benefit of his lust was her own well-maintained body—in as good shape as this twenty-something's. He seemed still to desire her, but had he contemplated divorce himself?

They shared sweets by the fireplace, Ben even feeding Liz a miniature creampuff. Suggestively? She led him back to the kitchen but could not help glancing back. Jenna was talking to others but her scouting eyes meant the connection remained unsevered.

Liz gathered more desserts for the porch and set the plate on a table in front of Margaret. Ben sank into the cushiony couch beside his mother. To two female cousins Margaret announced, "And here is Liz, even on this sad day caring for us. And, in the flesh, my boy Ben."

Years ago, Margaret seemed shocked when her baby boy was revealed to be an addict. She declared Liz a saint for sticking to the marriage vows. But she never ceased the enabling praise, elevating her offspring to a virile god. The woman was as addicted to bragging as Ben was to sex. "Tell them about Iraq." Ben had flown in the first Gulf War.

Ben gave Liz's hand a squeeze, small penance paid. Liz wondered at the connection of mother and son and its effect on Ben's condition. Margaret fed his narcissism. Ben began every quest for self with much to prove. Sex, both seduction and act, became compulsive, disordered. Even as he talked about airstrikes, hardened bunkers, a fallen comrade, his tales seemed ritualistic, his excitement practiced. But Liz was no longer addicted. Having delivered him from Jenna, she'd done enough today to preserve their marriage. Had they all forgotten what the day meant for her?

Liz left the glassed porch by the stairs to the yard. Neither Ben nor Margaret acknowledged her departure. When mother and son were together, Liz went unnoticed. She surveyed the garden, abandoned for the several weeks she'd tended to her father's final illness. The deer had been here all right, and rabbits too. Who knew what other creatures foraged in a drought year? The tomato plants were rumpled, the squash leaves gnawed, the beans picked clean. She felt herself untended and used. She'd stuck by Ben through counseling, his weeks in rehab facilities, group meetings with other spouses, all intended to break any chain of codependency. Had her attraction to his god-image and his flattering interest somehow served her own needs? More likely—and she had thought about this a lot—her good-daughterliness, her wish to please, some desire for attention, even if scandalous, drove her. But she'd survived.

A muggy breeze blew in from the lake and something stirred

in the woods. She shook her head at the wasted garden—let the scavengers come—and went back inside. Sister-in-law Charlene had replaced Ben on the porch, laughing with Margaret. These two surely must be bored by funeral duty by now. What new topics had they taken up—Ben's seduction of Charlene's *stepdaughter*? Surely she'd warned the girl off. But where were the lovebirds now?

Before Liz could go inside to search, Margaret waved her over. "I'm so glad you aren't planning to sell this wonderful house. You know how much Ben loves it."

Charlene ahemed and Liz caught her look. "As does everyone. Maybe the family will keep it for vacations?" They must have been discussing the will.

Her father's house sat only three hundred yards from the Lake Michigan beach. A golf-cart path cut through the woods onto the rolling dunes. It wasn't the house she'd grown up in. Her father was hardly sentimental and the minute he could afford it—kids out of college—had moved from Hammond over her mother's qualms into this extravagance. Ben had helped with the search. Now all of them associated the property with the vacation lifestyle her dad embraced when he retired, more so after her mother died. He'd thrived on his new leisure as much as he had his work.

"Oh, Charlene, we can't be making those decisions right now."

No kidding, Liz thought. Not you, dear mother-in-law, or you, sister-in-law, merely the wife of my long-dead brother, remarried to that little man whose name everyone forgets, who makes big money as a tax attorney. What do you care? My father's house should be mine.

"Uncle Terrance is the executor," Liz informed them. Her dad's responsible brother.

"He'll help us sort everything out before probate." It occurred to Liz that Charlene might be due for a third of the estate, Mark's third. Would she have to share this house with Charlene and what's-his-name ... and Jenna? Might Margaret become a permanent summer guest?

Charlene and Margaret dithered, their greed showing. Liz felt some plot afoot to take her world from her. In the kitchen the crowd thinned and the living room showed no sign of Ben or Jenna. Liz's sons, James and Kyle, sat in a corner exhausted. All afternoon they'd greeted family friends outside and toted food in. Let us represent, they said, meaning, you watch dad and deal with the relatives. They'd never been their father's keepers—Liz's tough love insisted on their escape from Ben's condition. But in many ways, Ben's addiction had replaced—stolen—her own life.

She checked the garage and killed time straightening the kitchen. She'd bought too much food and questioned the etiquette of sending home care packages from a wake. The booze had taken a substantial hit, especially the good wine. Still, when they got around to culling her father's artifacts, there'd be liquor to help her through. She anticipated the need to escape. She set out clean glasses and headed down the hall toward the bedrooms. If, in her father's house, on the day of his funeral, with his mother, not to mention his children and his wife so close at hand, he'd brought the girl, nearly a relative, back here ... well, no court would convict her.

Liz entered the nearest bedroom, the one she'd used while caring for her father. Sun created shadows through drawn curtains.

Arranged on a chest of drawers, photos of herself and her siblings seemed glyphs of another life. As children they'd played in the small fenced yard of the city house. Fortunate thanks to her father, secure under her mother's eyes. But heading for what futures? Mark's early death, Lynette's distance. Her own hopes rocked by Ben's compulsion. Liz looked at the bed. How many times had she and Ben had sex there, made love. If she fell asleep, would anyone come looking for her in this room, in this house she could hardly call her own?

She sat on the bed. Tears came and she tightened her eyes. She heard a clatter against the wall. And little sputters, words muted into coughs. The bastard was fucking the little bitch, up against the wall or pressed onto the headboard. It sounded like a muffled fight for domination, the way he liked it when driven, as if one more thrust of hip, one more clamp of hand, another desperate moan, would set him free. She dizzied and prayed for his release. When the sounds ceased, Liz imagined Ben's grin, Jenna's sigh, and wanted to be outside, to join the deer, to forage in the garden's detritus.

She waited ten minutes after the adjacent door clicked closed then reapplied makeup. She would reappear, as her normal self.

Margaret still regaled Charlene—the little husband settled beside her—and a flushed Jenna who squinted in the slanting sun. Liz could easily lower the blinds on the west side, but she enjoyed the sun's glare as a weapon. She would not play victim.

Ben remained absent, probably outside the garage sneaking a cigarette. Sex energized rather than sapped him—the rush lasted hours. At home, finished with Liz, he'd bolt to his man-cave, spin the fancy globe she'd bought him, search exotic destinations, his close-to-home world never enough. Even released, he could not escape his compulsion. Did her patience enable him?

She nodded past family and friends that weren't really hers and went to the garden. She looked over a patch she'd turned back to earth last week as her father declined. Sore muscles, sweat, and distraction. Liz inhaled a mix of sandy soil and musty lake. She imagined the water, a horizon that seemed vast. Her legs wobbled. They hadn't become boat people though docks were nearby. Her father preferred to fish from the community pier, catching a bit of peace. She'd sometimes joined him. Or perhaps now she'd dive beneath the surface to find renewal.

Dry brush rustled and Liz saw two deer, a doe and fawn, staring at her from the woods. Nothing leafy remained to pick in their yard. The deer looked miserable, huge eyes unblinking. It had been a hard year on them, too. She bent down and yanked a fruitless pepper plant from the ground, held out its roots toward them.

Both deer twitched then bolted in a flash of brown. How did they move so fast in the thicket? She wanted to run after them, through the dark grove to the beach.

"Were those the deer?" Margaret, snuck up behind her, asked. "Worthless plot. Did they do that?" The brown earth suddenly reminded Liz of her father's grave. "In Georgia, we'd use raised beds with wire around them." She smiled and tapped Liz's elbow. "Someone needs to be here to keep it up. Who's got the greenest thumb?" They both knew that only Mark had inherited her father's true interest in gardening. But Ben often bragged he loved planting, too, more than the cultivation or harvest.

Charlene plodded down the porch steps as Jenna stood in the doorway, framed by glassy sunbursts as if she were on fire. "Why, Liz, people are leaving," Charlene said as she neared. She looked aghast at the wasted plants. "My God, how'd you let this bed go to pot? I'm glad Mark isn't here to see this mess."

"Now, Charlene," Margaret said, "Liz isn't to blame. She was here to take care of her dad, not the garden." Even her solicitude condescended. "Ben would clean it up, if he moved in here." Her eyes swept the yard. Ben claimed to love the house and certainly loved the lake. Thank God Margaret would have no say in dividing the estate.

"Well, I can't stand to look at it." Charlene backed away so quickly Liz thought she might trip on the uphill slope. "Liz, I'm sorry, but we have to go." Though Char managed not to stumble, Liz saw Jenna tense on the stairs as Ben appeared behind her shoulder. "When's the probate? We'll all getting together again then, I suppose?" Would she drag the girl along to the hearing?

Charlene heaved across the yard and up the steps. Next to Margaret Liz felt unsteady, unprepared for whatever might come next. Jenna moved away from Ben, waved a weak goodbye to all, with a guilty look at Liz. Ben kept smiling.

Margaret said, "Liz, you need to go in and say goodbyes. Don't leave that to Ben and the boys."

Liz stiffened. "I'll be coming along, Margaret. I need another minute alone."

Her mother-in-law's gaze seemed wicked with pity before she marched uphill and through the porch door.

Liz turned to the woods. Nothing moved. No cool wind from

the west, no scent of chlorophyll from the lake. She wished her father would appear to tell her how to reclaim her life. The garden held only brown plants, dry earth. She knelt and raked the hard soil with her nails. She looked back up to the house, taken over by so many strangers it might as well be empty.

———————

PUPPIES 4 SALE

No takers since the mid-afternoon drunk who'd crunched the curb when he pulled over. The little dogs had moaned and scratched the travel crate in fear. Monte first refused to sell to him, then figured business was business. "Puppies 4 Sale" his sign offered. Total for two days—five dogs sold, three to go. Monte sat on the concrete steps, one arm rested on the metal mesh while the other waved a cigarette in the air whenever a car slowed. Traffic was thin on State Street today, his last with this litter. Food cost him the humiliation of scavenging scraps at Kate's Café or behind the Village Pantry east on Prospect. If they didn't sell, after dark he'd drown the dogs—he refused to call them puppies except with clients.

Few of those nearby though the neighborhood stayed busy, rehabs and new restaurants a few blocks over near Fountain Square, and especially down at the corner where the latest renovation picked up speed. Monte saw the money guy who'd bought three of the four corners—the brick buildings—surveying the exterior handiwork on the one that neared completion. The next block north he watched his once friend Sandi, now a red-haired meth whore in ripped jeans, wiggling her scrawny hips beside a bus stop as if some stranger might descend and buy. But her skanky tit-tats and wobbly platforms were no more enticing than her bad teeth. Monte wondered how a man could allow his dick to enter such decay. He'd told her "no" several times since he'd gotten off the meth himself after two despairing weeks dabbling with it. While he couldn't say he felt in all ways cured yet, at least he could enjoy the sunshine on his bare arms without scratching, or squinting to avoid seeing the world around him for what it was. Eyes open it was pretty damned crappy, but the neighborhood was his reality, his life.

The dogs whimpered and he almost broke down to scratch one little nose pushed through the wire. The renovator man paced toward him as if measuring the empty lot between his building and Monte's house. "Shush up," Monte told the dogs. "You'd eat good with this guy, believe me." He gentled the carrier like a cradle then stood.

He couldn't remember the money man's name but tried to smile. About thirty like Monte, he'd power-washed the ancient two-story so the brick came clean and sharp-edged. He'd put in new doors—at the back wooden ones with mosaic patterns and, on the front, silvery scroll work and hinges shaped like Arabian swords. Above that door he'd placed a limestone wolf's head. The bastioned battlement around the roof's edge made the place look like a fortress.

Mr. Money hollered, "Hey, brother," giving a two-fingered salute. His step quickened and Monte remembered the name—Travis, like a traveling salesman. His work clothes, cowhide carpenter pants and suspenders over a flannel shirt, remained unstained even in the heat. But at least he was doing a lot of the building work himself, so they had something in common. Last year, when Monte lost the gopher job at the woodworking plant he'd hoped would lead to an apprenticeship, he got right back to work building the "kennel" behind the house he'd inherited from his mother, his single legacy. Only his ex-girlfriend Vicky "helped." They even made a stab at putting up a high wood fence until he realized that if the posts weren't cemented the whole thing would fall. He realized that, of course, only when it happened.

Travis put out his hand and Monte took it tentatively. "I got some cute puppies here, mister … Travis," he stammered, embarrassed at the guy's quick shake and dismissal.

Travis peered into the cage, hopefully attracted by their unusual features. The dogs yelped in relief from their boredom. Monte hoped they sounded like good property guardians.

Monte had no idea what work was still going on inside the building, but knew that Travis also bought Sammy's Saloon nearby, long closed despite its notoriety as a 20s honkytonk speakeasy. Signs of the past were easily forgotten in these parts. Kitty-corner from the reno, a carved limestone "F. & A. M." still ID'ed the three-story Masonic lodge that now housed a used clothes store and crappy studio apartments.

One of the tenants there, a puffy woman in a Black Sabbath t-shirt, neared them pushing a stroller. She said, "Say 'hi' to the neighbors, honey," and both Monte and Travis nodded to the toddler, who sported a mullet. The tyke rode bare-chested and surly-looking, concentrating on the Popsicle he grasped like a prize. The dogs quieted and the kid said nothing. The woman shrugged and walked on.

Travis, like Monte, barely contained his laughter. "Man, that's some hairdo on a baby. Travis giggled into his hand. "Our neighbors," he said. "At least until next October."

So the Masonic building would be emptied and redone, too. Travis had supposedly encouraged the going out of business sale at the Used Tire Depot that filled the fourth corner. Who knew what so-called progress might develop there if the public housing project under debate for that block fell through? Restaurants he'd never afford or a Starbucks for people with time to waste.

Monte smiled as if the idea of change made him happy and Travis asked him to bring one of the dogs out into the light. Monte fiddled with the lock and their tongues gooed up his knuckles. His skin was still touchy after four weeks clean. Thank God he'd wised up before he ended like Sandi. He grabbed one of the dogs by its scruff and closed the door on the other two. "This one's got the spirit."

Travis petted between the dog's big ears. Monte figured he might not want as much fight in his dogs as most people in the neighborhood. "But the patience of an angel, too," quoting something his mom once said about him.

Monte held the little dog so its legs kicked. Its coat shone in the sunshine, short yellow-brown fur. Wind up around forty-fifty pounds, but tough with shepherd and terrier in the mix. "Here, you hold him. Cute guy's not a biter."

Travis took a step back and eyed the dog all around as if examining a statue. "I need a watch dog for the building while we finish the upstairs' lofts." He waved his hand back and forth in the dog's face. To see how the eyes tracked, Monte guessed.

He bounced the dog a little, to shake out more reaction, but it cooed and drooled, not a single yip or nip. "Oh, he's gotta lot of life, mister. Just woke up from a nap. "Full shepherd."

Travis tightened his mouth. "Part maybe." He petted the dog's rump, then pulled his hand away and wiped it on his thigh.

"Or I've got another bitch ready to drop that's part pit bull." Another month before he could sell any of those potential killers. He'd regretted borrowing the ill-tempered stud when he witnessed its aggressive mating.

Travis chuckled. "I don't think so, bud." He scanned down State in Sandi's direction, as if the next block might make good property for him. He grimaced when he caught sight of the girl, who gave a come-hither wave and bent over a bit so her tits showed white amidst the ink. "Christ," he muttered. "Maybe I should hire *her*. No one would dare break in on that."

Sandi took the attention as an invitation and staggered toward them, scratching her arm. Monte tensed. She wasn't a bad person, he reminded himself, or once hadn't been. Christ, they'd been kids together at McKinley Elementary when the new building opened. In fourth grade she'd kissed him by the swing set before she moved on to more experienced boys and other cities. Been a hairdresser or something. She'd come back home only to be kicked out by her parents. He wished he didn't know where she lived.

"Hey, Monte," she crooned. "Cute little puppies, huh, mister." Her words tripped out over ragged teeth. Red scabs dotted her cheeks and neck like measles. "Buy me a puppy, mister, and we'll be your friends for life." Even her girlish giggle mocked the real thing.

She reached toward Travis' arm, but he pulled back. "Sorry, sister, nothing for you." He drew himself up. "Except some advice."

Sandi raised her eyebrows and chuckled and Monte worried Travis might slap her. He stood in case he needed to step between them.

"You can get help at the Center," Travis said, referring to the new community center a few blocks north across Washington Street where renovation work continued—of people as well as buildings—making that neighborhood feel better, at least for the moment. "All you have to do is walk in the door and ask."

Sandi snorted and glared, but at Monte, not Travis who turned his back on her. She pushed her lips together in a fake kiss. "You assholes have a nice day, you hear." She spat on the ground toward Monte. "You got cute puppies, Monte. Glad you made some friends." She scowled then stalked away.

Travis stretched his shoulders. "Don't think I'll be hiring *that* for anything." He again scanned the dog. "And I can't use your dog, either. Sorry, buddy."

Monte sat down and brought the dog into his lap. "But maybe you could hire me." He straightened. "I'm tougher than I look." He scratched behind the dog's ears. "I'm about done with this puppy business." It was true. He was making bread money, not mortgage. He didn't want to go back to working the pick-up crews with men in worse shape than him, or selling dope. Working for this asshole would be a new start. He restrained the wriggling dog easily, his muscle tone rebuilding, more beefed up considering his distance from poor Sandi's fall.

Travis towered over him, scanning Monte like he had the dog. "Dude, you are skin and bones." He scanned Monte's house as well. "But maybe you could sell this place to me. Must be a lot for you to take care of."

Monte thought his house not so bad, paint chipped and shingles faded but gutters unbent. Plenty around here had weathered worse. His mother had put pride into it, and their neighborhood where people looked out for one another. Now most of her generation were dead or moved. It didn't matter. He had no place else to go and the mortgage crisis made his lender forgiving, seemingly unaware that investors like Travis might take interest in the decay.

"Nah, I been in here three years since my Mom died. And this is my neighborhood since I was a kid." Travis wasn't giving, so he might as well push back. "Besides, you Fountain Square bigshots think you're improving the neighborhood so much, my house might really be worth a few bucks to you before long."

Travis snickered. "Oh, so happy to give you folks some hope." He reached out—Monte feared to punish his insolence—but only tapped the dog's head and turned away.

Good riddance, Monte thought. Whose renewal was this urban renewal stuff anyway? The guy hadn't dealt with despair one second of his life. Monte opened the crate and scooted the dog back inside. He wondered how soon the whole corner would advertise "lofts" or "flats." The business renovations seemed never to end and the little houses built on half-lots in the early 1900s were thinned out by foreclosure and demolition all the way over to Fountain Square.

The dogs shuffled around on their oversized paws. Monte rocked the cage and squinted after Travis who stood in the weedy lot reading a newly planted plastic sign titled "New Public Housing—Hearing Sunday." He pulled the invitation from the ground, rolled it into a wand, and used the metal stumps to poke the ground. Then he sniffed the air.

He called back to Monte. "Man, I can smell your dogs from here. You're gonna have to do something about that." Travis gave a thumbs-up and nodded as if he assumed Monte's agreement. He turned on his heels like a soldier, marched to his building, and disappeared inside.

Now that Monte smelled for it, he found plenty of dog in the air—so what? He rattled the crate and the three dogs whimpered at his anger. "Like hell I'll get rid of you," he whispered.

Up the street Sandi sat against a spindly tree. Weeds nearly covered her body, her once-pretty face showing like a dried flower. Monte squinted. They were all refugees in their own neighborhood. He couldn't offer his spare room, but he'd walk her to the community center. Otherwise she might disappear into the haze he'd almost entered until the litter's birth returned his sense of responsibility. He'd watched their mother nurse them, her irritation growing until Monte started to wean them. Brushed them. Petted them. Scratched their ears and in the empty lot buried the runt that died.

Monte wiped his eyes, sore and moist. He rocked the carrier and the puppies woofed. He talked back to them, promising that even if he had to move, he'd find each one a good home.

PYRAMID SCHEME

T HE MANSION'S OWNER, MR. HARRIS, IS CHECKING my work again, fourth time today. This safe room my boss Settle and I are building for him. He gauges the vaulted doorframe, the drywall hiding steel like smooth limestone masked the rough blocks of ancient pyramids. Harris sneers at me like I'm some pharaoh's slave.

He's into Egypt big time, like I was in middle school. Glass cases show off his collection—figurines, amulets, painted potsherds. But downstairs there's another secret room—reached via a panel in the library—that Settle built last year to protect precious, and my bet illegal, artifacts. I've snuck in there though its chill creeps me out. Papyrus scrolls, golden scarabs, god-headed staffs, a mummy's sarcophagus—without the mummy, thank Isis! On one wall that crazy old artist Taft (he who newsworthily drowned in the estate's pond) painted a mural with the god Horus's head replaced by Harris's own hawk-like face! The man is obsessed—with Egypt and himself.

We'll be finished tomorrow, Settle reminds him. My last day on any job? We've been at it two months, but last week I got this feeling from Harris's look that something was off. He's the type who'd as soon kill me as scowl. I said this to Settle who laughed at my concern, clapped me on the back like I'm his buddy. But really there's no one who'd much miss me. Settle deposits Harris's checks and cuts me cash. He's dependent on these rich guys, as were those architects for the pyramids, right? I'm mere labor and could quit anytime, just not show up, but it would be my last day of any work anywhere up here in ritzy Hamlin County. Times are tough since the union died and Settle reminds me I'm lucky to be the help here—so don't be a hindrance. Guess I'll wait for my pay and see what turns up next.

Harris smirks as if he'd actually recognize quality work. "Good job, Settle, and almost on time." He gives a thumbs-up as he glances at me. Settle gives me a nod as he follows Harris out. But left alone, I don't feel safe in his safe room.

A "safe" room—safe from what? I put on the mask and open the paint can. Harris's a big shot, smiles photogenic in the paper though he's skinny and bald. Arts gigs mostly, "benefits" that guys like me see no benefit from. His friends might be jealous, but no one except the IRS poses danger to more than his ego. Only losing wealth causes alarm. I mean the estate has armed guards. And there aren't a lot of Egyptian art thieves around except in movies. Kidnap his over-bleached wife or chubby college son? Who could stand them long enough to collect the ransom? Harris claims to be a self-made man but some say his business is nothing but a Ponzi … a pyramid scheme so to speak!

The paint fumes burn my eyes and haze my vision. These walls would quickly close in on me all alone, even if I was as rich as

Harris. The room's empty now, but even equipped with comfort and cameras, such safety seems twisted. No marble bathroom with gold fixtures can shine up the windowless gloom.

Fear of anything outside himself, maybe that's it, security for its own sake—one small step from paranoia. Like Pharaoh feared the Jews, or Pilate feared Jesus. Some omen Harris sees in our stained clothes and weathered faces, as if we threaten him with some sturdy silence he wants to control. If I fought back—against what?—there'd be no winning. Better to let this chamber be a giant canopic burial jar to store Harris's cold heart.

I shake my head to clear the giddy vapors, but keep painting. After this only cleanup's left. Settle will stay on, overseeing the dig for a weather shelter beneath the six-car garage. A tornado this spring took tiles off the roof and apparently tizzied Mrs. Harris like she'd been bitten by an asp. Other projects loom down the road—a basketball barn, a second guest house, an infinity pool the size of infinity. Mr. Harris's got 200 acres and his own golf course following the creek that wends like the Nile through his empire, so the possibilities seem endless. Settle will have work here for life! I only hope he calls me back when the new construction starts.

The big boss looks in again to see how I'm doing. Holding his nose he *does* look like Horus, a uniquely ugly superstar. I heard rumors he may run for office, Mayor or even Governor. Con or not, Harris's so rich he must know things I don't. Maybe I'd vote for him and let the wealth trickle down to me. What would I have to lose?

He directs Settle to the unfinished wall, painting strokes in the air before he backs out. Settle nods at me, exits, then shuts the door tight. He's not a bad guy. I'll work for him again in a second if I get the chance. So I tidy up a corner and move to the final wall, the narrow one beside the bathroom door. I feel like I'm moving slowly, the closed air heavy with the paint's reek. My brush moves in slow motion from can to wall until I find my pace, a rower on a barge, bondsman fanning with a palm. There's no use arguing with the gods, old ones or new.

My vision is dizzy, but the job looks pretty good. A sandish gold that compliments the floor's tile. Other colors swirl in my eyes. What special pieces from his collection will Harris hold here, precious as himself? I wonder what vessel will store his soul, and picture him hiding here, scared as the rest of us, trapped and waiting for his end. I tremble to think of such a life without death, so secure, a corpse preserved for all eternity.

———◆———

LITTLE JUNGLE

THE BOTTLE BROKE AGAINST THE BOULDER AND gasoline spread flames onto the dry grass, then slow-burned toward the brush and trees at the clearing's edge, more fire than Matt had expected. His friend Lewis, only nine to Matt's eleven, whimpered beside him. His cell phone hung dead in his pocket. Lewis's parents invested their money to spoil his teenage sister Leah, so he had no phone at all. Some of the brush caught fire. Even if Matt could get home to call the fire department before the Little Jungle burned down, his life would be going up in flames, too. Making the Molotov cocktail was all his idea. He'd read about the weapon in his dad's history books, but he hadn't imagined this result. A dry reed flamed up. What had his supposedly great imagination ever earned him?

The summer so far seemed an exercise in stupidity if not outright badness. His mother had taken a bookkeeping job and now both parents worked except weekends. He guessed they considered his getting to 6th grade some rite of passage and let him run wild. He and Lewis were the only kids who really played outside any more. Early in June, Matt stayed up in some mulberry trees in the Jungle all one afternoon, stuffing himself with juicy berries like the birds did. He came home with red-stained hands to a supper he couldn't stomach and puked half the night. "You should have known better," his mother said. His father laughed at the breakfast table when Matt took two bites of toast and his face turned sour again. He really was on his own.

Now Matt surveyed the fire's spread and tried to think while Lewis hopped like a chicken with its head cut off. The grass around the boulder looked like black fuzz, but the flames slowed where the ground went mushy by a thicket of weedy trees. It might have been worse if he'd tossed the burning bottle at the broken farm wagon he'd first targeted. It sat collapsed over its wheels, wood decayed but dry as tinder.

Anyway, Leah had already turned the wagon meaningless for Matt last summer when she came out to bring Lewis home. She ruined the tale he'd told Lewis—how the wagon came from Morgan's Raiders' Civil War attack on Indiana. But look, Leah had said, rubber tires. She was four years older, and far more reasonable. Lewis waited for Matt to argue, but there was nothing to say. Leah looked at Matt like he was the world's biggest dope.

Putting out the fire themselves would save both face and explanations. He signaled Lewis to help stomp out flare-ups around the boulder. That was easy. He emptied his backpack of candy and juice, no water, and walked closer to the fire's spread.

At least he no longer felt like hiding. Last summer he and Lewis had played sheriff and outlaw with the authentic toy Colt 45 Matt's dad passed along for his birthday. Lewis thought you hit the guy with the plastic butt end of the gun, but Matt knew better—you used the metal barrel, like this! Lewis ran home bleeding and Matt ran crying to his room. I'm sorry, he said to no one but maybe God until his mother found him and said Lewis would be all right, just apologize. At the hospital they used a dozen stitches to close the wound. Lewis's mother had glared at Matt like he was the outlaw. And so had Leah.

Now he yelled at Lewis to stay away. All he needed was the kid to go up in smoke. Matt flailed his backpack at the brush. The thick weeds sent a gray fog into the blue sky, the smell choking. He coughed and backed away. He thought, you can't put out smoke, and looked for the bursts of actual fire.

He had good vision, they told him, and he'd tested it himself. They'd taken away his toy Colt—"Too old for this, aren't you?"— so he'd rounded up his dad's old BB gun from the garage. From his favorite mulberry tree he spotted a robin fifty feet away. He sighted on the bird's fat chest and pulled the trigger. Matt thought the BB would just send it flying, but the bird swung on the branch like a midway target then fell to the ground, dead as a doornail. He felt sorry, and was glad Lewis hadn't seen that—he might have cried.

Now he hoped there weren't any birds or animals trapped by the fire. That would be a horrible way to die. Matt looked back to make sure Lewis kept his distance.

He kicked some of the sandy ground at the blaze and some smoke settled, so he scooped handfuls onto where the fire must be hiding, but it wasn't enough. He ran back to Lewis and began to shovel the pebbly stuff into his backpack. He told Lewis to fill up his bag, too.

The boy froze. "Maybe we should go get Leah."

Matt shook his head 'no way.' If he had an enemy in the world, it was Leah. She'd actually babysat Matt last year—as if he still needed a babysitter. She switched the TV to the Kardashians, texting or making calls, complaining she was stuck watching a brat for money. Matt was surprised how much you could learn about a person listening to them jabber. He wished he could've read her texts, but didn't dare hijack her phone when she went into the kitchen—which was often. She rifled through the refrigerator, leaving the door open longer than his mom would have approved. Still, though she told him he could play in his room or watch TV in the basement, he didn't leave the living room. Instead, he watched the way she twisted her hair and fiddled nervously with her clothes.

But now Lewis depended on him to act. He hoped the Little Jungle's mushy ground made things wet enough the fire couldn't spread, but in the thicket more flames flared near taller trees and he felt his bad luck had struck again.

Lewis said, "Please, Matt, I'll go get her."

Matt looked sternly at Lewis and tugged his backpack until the boy bent down and pushed sandy pebbles in. Then Matt moved toward the fire, making sure Lewis stayed behind him. The flames gave off heat as well as smoke, not a good sign. The closest brush crackled, burnt black. He leaned in to find the flames then raised the pack over his head and shook out the gravel. The little rocks clattered into the brush, caught the edges of the fire, and slowed things down. Matt yelled at Lewis to trade packs and go back to refill Matt's. Then he emptied Lewis' smaller bag and the flames stalled. This would work if they could get enough sand into the trees.

Lewis was still scooping as Matt had the smaller bag refilled. "We gotta go fast." Matt took over filling the larger bag. He pushed the small bag to Lewis. "Haul this over there. Make like a fire brigade."

They'd have to stick together, like he was always telling Lewis. A couple of weeks ago, they took up spy positions behind the propane tank in Lewis's backyard as Leah dressed for some party. Wrapped in a towel, she held up a bra and panties as if matching them. When she dropped the towel, Matt let out a huge sigh then caught his breath. Lewis punched his arm and said they shouldn't be watching. Matt told Lewis not to watch if he didn't want to, but after all Lewis had told her schedule. Leah stretched as she turned to look out the window and her breasts stared right at Matt despite the distance. He knew he couldn't be visible in the shadows but he flinched and closed his eyes. He didn't want to be bad in that way, too. When Matt forced his eyes open she was fastening the bra. Lewis hit him again and pleaded, "Now can we go?" For days after that Lewis frowned when Matt asked how Leah was doing.

Matt took only a few seconds to finish the big backpack, but Lewis screamed. The boy was holding his arms over his head, the small bag on fire. "Jesus Christ, Lewis, drop it!"

The kid froze and Matt rushed, tackled him so the pack stuck in the brush as they went down. Lewis started crying and Matt looked for some sign of burns. Nothing looked like a scald or blister but soot covered Lewis's hands and arms. Matt dared run his hands over the skin and Lewis didn't cringe. Only ash from the burned bushes, he prayed.

"You idiots!" someone shouted. Matt looked up and Leah charged at them. "Pull him away." The flames hissed and sputtered in the thicket as he helped Lewis to his feet. Leah hefted up a red extinguisher, tugged its silver switch, and blasted a white cloud onto the fire until it flickered out. She moved around, stomping the burned brush down to find lingering flares and blast them. Sirens blared far away, heading their direction.

Lewis wiggled his fingers testing for injury. Matt could tell he wasn't burned even a bit. Lewis looked at Matt for only a second, then ran to his sister as she stood with the red can in one hand, her other arm open to welcome Lewis. For Matt her look was all accusation. "You stupid punk." Lewis hugged her waist and didn't look at Matt. "You ought to be locked up." Leah looked back across the grassy field, past the mulberry trees to 14th street.

Two fire trucks pulled up then the smaller truck came bouncing across the field toward them. Leah backed Lewis away to the other side of the boulder. Lewis, probably Matt's former friend now, might get a ride to the hospital, sent there again by Matt's hand. Maybe he *would* be locked up—firebug, arsonist. Maybe he *should* be.

He said "I'm sorry" a dozen times as the firemen bounded off the truck then hosed down the thicket, sent smoke into the sky, and hacked down what was left. One guy was talking to Leah and Lewis. Both of them pointed at Matt, Leah's look still scornful, Lewis scared and sad.

Matt leaned against the splintery wagon, his hand on one of the stupid rubber wheels. He looked up at the smoke as it turned into white wisps in the blue sky. The man in big black boots stomped toward him while Leah and Lewis huddled beyond. "I'm sorry," Matt said, wondering if he'd need to keep saying it forever. "I'm sorry, really sorry."

SHELTER

1976

ICRANKED OPEN THE GREMLIN'S WINDOW AND THE charry smell
from Burger Chef and McDonald's made my mouth water.
Near noon on a bright October day and me and the boy hadn't
eaten breakfast. Aaron stood on the seat. "Burgers, Randy! It's just
a shot away!"

I liked how he borrowed from my favorite song, but I gave him
the stern grownup look—we didn't have money to spare for junk
until I picked up the stuff to make some new deals.

He hooted like a monkey. "Peggy won't know." He knew how
to work me. "I won't tell."

I pulled into McDonald's knowing full well that Peggy *would*
figure it out between her mom radar and good nose. There'd be a
lecture for me and a smack on the ass for Aaron. She never lets
him off the hook for my bad judgment, but Ari's not my kid, so
there's not much I can do about it. And she doesn't respond well to
threats. And since avoiding Viet Nam, I'm a man of peace myself.

I walked around to his door and he jumped into my arms with

his sweet child scent and kissed my cheek like I was his favorite man in the world, though I doubted that was true. Peggy's most recent ex, Michael, aka Peter Pan—not Aaron's dad, either—had favorite man territory staked out. But I knew Aaron wanted to be carried so I hefted him over my shoulder and limped into the restaurant pretending I was a hunchback.

I ordered him a McDonaldland "Fun-To-Go meal, *to stay*," and the girl at the counter smiled big. Someone got my sense of humor. There wasn't much joking at our place of late. I let Aaron pay and the little Hamburglar pocketed the change. At the table, he made quick work of the fries but picked off the pickle, getting mustard on his fingers, ketchup on his knuckles. I made him wait for the prize until he'd chowed down most of the burger.

The toy was Grimace in the form of a pen-topper, still a purple blob, hardly a real prize. Aaron looked thoughtful. Michael had bought him a set of artsy pencils, one of his "learning tool" bribes. He'd been buying the boy's love since last October when Aaron's acting dad Robert—not the actual husband/father Peggy claimed was one of the last men shot dead in Vietnam—brought him from Florida to Michael's rented farmhouse. Peggy'd been living there just a few months.

Then this spring, Peggy and I hit it off at the parts plant before we got laid off. She offered me the spare bedroom at the farm. They needed money and she needed company. So our "family" drama began. That act ended in six weeks—Peggy and the kid getting the duplex with me, Michael left alone to finish his last month of grad school. Now he remained the odd-man-out third wheel in our adult triangle, but the fourth wheel stabilizing the family.

He still paid most of Aaron's expenses. Confusing? Sometimes I wonder if the kid really knows who to love.

Aaron wiped his mouth with his sleeve—the stain would mean more anger. I say, let the boy be a boy. Peggy comes back, "Why, so he'll grow up like you?"

In the restroom, I helped him use the low urinal. "Pee like a man," he said Michael called it. Peggy had him pee sitting down. You had to take care with his clothes then hold his shoulders to aim his stub into the basin. I tried to recall how I'd learned, but I only remembered the big trough urinal at a Tiger Stadium ballgame one of my mom's boyfriends took me to when I was little. Aaron managed pretty well this time. Underwear up, pants up, snap snapped, good to go. I helped him wash at the sink, but the stain on his sleeve was not coming out.

Back in the parking lot, I remembered the real point of our journey—to Zoe and Rag's for a big bag of their fresh-off-the-boat no-shit-about-it Panama Red.

When we got to our duplex, after 1:00, Peggy was still taking care of business in our bedroom. I sat Aaron on the couch, brought a wooden bowl from the kitchen to the coffee table, poured the dope in, and set him to sorting out seeds while I picked out stems.

I rolled a joint and the sweet-sour smell filled the room until I opened a window. Aaron looked pale, so I tucked the blue comforter Michael had given him around his legs.

Michael was supposed to pick Aaron up at 2:00 like every Saturday. On Wednesdays he took him overnight after the social worker's visit, always bringing something Aaron needed that we lacked. But as angry as he often looked, Michael never complained about how we lived, maybe because he knew Peggy would shear his balls! Everything was a stalemate. We needed the time off from the kid as well as the money and gifts, and Peggy'd been called to Child Services for counseling. Michael's help made us look good, or at least better.

We were making progress cleaning the grass when Michael arrived early. He came into the living room in his jean jacket and boots and gave us a look to kill, no doubt because of the marijuana, like he'd never toked up himself. He's a good-looking guy if you like hippie-teacher types and I understood Peggy's hooking him. He could take care of her thanks to his folks' money, but free-thinking as he pretended to be, there was lots of middle-class crap in that boy's head. He was book smart but street stupid not to have seen Peggy's routine—a classic on-the-road-damsel-in-distress. Even though Peggy's got twice the schemer's brains as me, I'd caught her game, but hell, her power turned me on. And I wanted to see what would happen next.

I said, "Michael, he's almost ready to go." Getting out from under the comforter, Aaron bumped the table and nearly spilled the bowl of seeds. I growled, "Careful, bub," and Michael dashed over to Aaron and lifted him up, comforter and all.

"Time to go, buddy," he said. "Now that your job's done." Michael shook his head like I was pathetic.

I stood up. "What do ya need for tonight, boss?" I aimed 'boss' at Aaron, but hoped Michael got the jab meant for him. I headed to Aaron's tiny room for his stuff. I'd packed the clothes and toys last night while Peggy was still out partying.

At that moment the guy Peggy had brought home chose to depart our bedroom. He wore a sport coat, tie hanging out from the pocket. They'd stumbled in at 3:30 from The Big Apple, the bar where she worked her sideline. A mix of the town's business types and college kids drank there, all of them thinking they were pool sharks, pinball wizards, and ladies' men.

The guy eyed me as Peggy came into the doorway, looking tired, strung out. She made sure I saw him hand her the cash. "Thanks a lot," he said.

"Maybe I'll see ya again," Peggy said. Her "weary of living" look was lots different from how she brightened at night. He smirked, meaning "not likely."

Peggy smirked back at him, and I went for Aaron's pack.

I followed the guy to the living room and to the door. He nodded at Michael who sized up what was happening. Michael rocked Aaron on his shoulder and hummed that sugary song he likes so much. "Even though we ain't got money," as if he'd ever gone without cash. Even the comforter was made by his mother. He was trying to keep Aaron from seeing the real world around him. A phony crock of shit.

He wouldn't look at me, though I wanted him to. This is me. A person just as much as you, I wanted to say. And I love the kid, too, man, I wanted to cry.

Then Peggy waltzed in—no attempt to make herself presentable. "How are you, Michael?" She shuffled into the kitchen to boil water for instant coffee. Not a word to Aaron. She was wearing last night's clothes. Tight jeans and the patchy cowgirl shirt she wears to play the innocent country girl. As if. She's from north Florida, here via Miami, and though I've listened to plenty of her stories, I don't think I've heard the truth about how and why she got to Ohio.

Michael glared like he could shoot her, but he's supposedly all non-violence like me. We'd talked, drinking beer at the farm before he caught us cheating, and I thought we might become friends despite other differences ... but that class shit never goes away. I'm pretty sure he sees me as white trash. Now with Aaron's pot-cleaning even more so.

"I would be fine, Peggy, if you'd act more like a mother." He sized up her outfit and I knew he wanted to add "and less like a whore." He wasn't interested in her as a partner anymore, but he still showed more than enough interest in Aaron. Maybe he just hated to give up, like the U.S. stuck on in 'Nam though the cause was obviously lost.

Peggy fake-pouted and spooned in the coffee. "But I *am* a mother, Michael, and you aren't anything here." She turned her back on him. "Go on, take him and get out." She patted Aaron on the head. "And you might get him out of that stained shirt at some point."

Aaron squirmed in Michael's arms. I hoped he wouldn't cry. Michael adjusted Aaron on his shoulder, picked up the bag. He brushed past me to the door. "I'll see you tomorrow, Randy, around four."

I held the screen open for them. "Okay, Michael." I patted Aaron on the back. "Bye, buddy. I love you. See you tomorrow."

Peggy muttered "good riddance" as they walked across the

muddy lawn. I saw Aaron's face, red and teary, thumb in his mouth. I ran out after them. "Michael," I called. "Maybe we can talk after you bring him back."

Michael looked at me, puzzled. He lifted Aaron up into the bucket seat and strapped him in. "Sure, Randy, anytime you want."

The rest of the day Peggy went on about how she had to get to Florida where her father, or ex Robert, might help us out. She blamed my lack of funds for her pick-up last night—he turned out to be pretty much a pig, she said, got rough when he saw the scarring on her shoulder from her bout with skin cancer.

I sold most of the dope quickly to the regular college boys and bikers. All you needed to do was clean the stuff, call it sinsemilla, and mark up the price. We went out late to The Detour Lounge where Peggy stuffed quarters in the jukebox to play every tune Hank Williams and Patsy Cline recorded. We laughed, and she pulled me onto the floor a couple of times to dance the honky-tonk. When Peggy was happy she was quite a girl.

Sunday, I woke about ten and watched some Jesus cartoon about sheep and sacrifice then ten minutes of a talk show discussing Viet Nam as if it hadn't ended a few years ago. Thank God I'd stayed out thanks to my scrawny bones. I sang, "If I don't get some shelter, I'm gonna fade away." Thanks to a high lottery number, Michael had shelter from the draft, real violence. I'd been fighting all my life and Michael claimed to have stood up at protests, but I wondered how things might be different if we'd been sent away to soldier.

Peggy stayed in bed late whether she was sleeping or not. She carried lots of stress, what with her promises to Robert who agreed to bring Aaron here only when she and Michael seemed solid. More promises to Michael and Child Services. More promises to me to make changes she knew must be made but so far couldn't handle. She avoided changing, then got caught and lied, then lied again about the lie. She'd even lied about getting up to make breakfast that morning.

So I scrambled eggs, toasted toast, and slathered it with grape jelly and percolated real coffee. I carried a plate and cup to the bedroom and shouldered the door open. The fork clattered to the floor and Peggy jolted up. "What?" Her eyes widened with fear but when she realized it was me, she glared, pulled the sheet over her breasts. "Leave me alone!"

As gently as I could, I said, "I made some breakfast for ya," and moved into the room.

She fell back into the sheets. "I don't want any breakfast." I sat beside her but she slid from me. "Bring me Aaron so we can sleep awhile together."

I sighed and set the plate on the floor. Peggy seemed groggy and I tried to rub her shoulders to ease her into the day. "Aaron's with Michael, baby. It's Sunday."

She let me rub. "That fucking bastard's trying to take my boy." I ground out a knot and she shuddered. "I'm getting out of here. You'll come with me. We'll drive your car and if it quits, we'll hitch from there." She huddled up fetal, and I felt the tension every-where I rubbed. "We can go today when he brings Aaron. Nothing here for us. This is all a mistake."

I held her shoulders. "Peggy, we can't go yet." She stiffened more. "They'd have the cops on us in a day. You see the therapist tomorrow and the caseworker comes Wednesday." They had us pretty much caged, depending on the calendar.

Peggy made a sound low in her throat, almost growling. "Then we'll go on Thursday. I've got to get out of fucking Ohio." She pulled from my hands and sat up. "Everybody wants to take that kid away from me. No more." Her teeth showed. "No, we get our checks on Friday, so we'll go Saturday. Now give me my breakfast."

I sat there while she ate, looking around at how little we'd have to pack. Aaron had more stuff in the next room than we had in here, but he'd settle for a few toys and the comforter. He was a good boy, really. Obedient. Quiet. I pictured him riding Michael's shoulder. Sad.

Peggy scarfed down the food. How would we eat on the road? Just enough money for gas and junk food with my unemployment and her children's aid. If need be, Peggy'd contribute the way she knew how, but every time she whored her anger grew. She hated those men. And when we got to Florida, what would her supposed saviors, father or Robert, make of me?

Peggy finished eating and rolled to the mattress. I didn't wait around for thanks and cleaned up in the kitchen. The house had to be presentable for Child Services' visit. I opened the windows to help clear out the stink.

Peggy was just out of the shower when Michael showed with Aaron at 4:00. She wore a heavy robe, her hair wrapped in a towel. I let them in and she offered Michael a cup of coffee. She picked Aaron up, kissed him a lot, and sang, "I'm so in love with you, honey." He kissed her too, but he kept glancing around, maybe confused. His eyes were too wide open.

Michael declined the coffee, patted Aaron's shoulder, and gave Peggy a half-hearted smile. He headed for the door and nodded for me to follow. Outside, we both lit up smokes. He said, "If you want to talk, I'll meet you at Kountry Kitchen in fifteen minutes." He looked like he'd decided something. I agreed and wondered if he saw me as a partner in whatever plan he'd dreamed up. He took broad steps to his van.

I told Peggy we needed groceries—I was scheduled to make chili mac for dinner—and asked if she needed anything else. Aaron said he wanted to go, but she hugged him even tighter and told me to get Virginia Slims and Little Debbie's. I breathed easy, tousled Aaron's hair, tried to give Peggy a peck on the cheek then breezed out the door.

I crossed the B&O tracks, passed the Little League and the V.F.W. The Kountry Kitchen Kafe rounded out the menu at the corner of Pappy's Garage, Smoke'n Gun head shop, and The Detour. I loved this real—no college—part of my hometown. I didn't want to leave. They'd call us back to the parts factory when business picked up again. We weren't union, but it was a decent job. Some guys had worked there thirty years. They'd tell you about the big war, World War II, even the Depression. They were proud and a couple families sent their kids to college, not to Viet Nam. Aaron'd grow up just fine in this town. If he wanted, later he could outgrow the place himself, without Peggy running away now.

Michael's red van was shiny in the lot, nearly new. Another

bonus from his parents over in Indiana. Lucky bastard. But he'd told me he often ate breakfast here and I was surprised as hell. I mean, they served grits and biscuits all day! Such things might have allied us if he'd given me a chance. Aaron trusted him. And we both loved the boy.

Michael waved me to the booth. He extended his hand but my arms tangled taking off my jacket. He waited until I could return the handshake, a solid grasp. "Sit down, sit, Randy," he said as if he was my host. The only other customers were two guys, one mohawk, one mullet, smoking with their coffee at the counter.

I buried myself in the menu though I knew I'd order the number 1: two eggs over easy, link sausages, hash browns, and all-American white bread toast! Was there anything better than having breakfast for lunch? Michael smiled. "Hey, I'm buying, man, get anything you want," like money might change my appetite.

The waitress brought a coffee pot and poured while we ordered, me first. Michael said, "Wow, I'll have what he's having, except make mine country ham." He nodded a lot, like I was a child who needed his approval.

"I love the food here," he said. "Used to come in after drinking, for grits to soak up the Scotch." I grinned. No doubt we'd sat there at different tables, each wishing he'd gotten lucky with a girl instead of eating grits, soused and lonely at three in the morning. Peggy had hooked Michael by putting on her gypsy personality to become exactly who he was looking for.

Michael stirred the sugar into his coffee. "How are things at home, Randy? Got the hang of Ari's routines yet?" He watched me closely. "Keeping him out of her range?"

SHELTER

I told him some of the stuff Aaron and I did together, like sneaking McDonald's and watching Little League and tossing a plastic ball. The waitress brought our meals and I stirred the yolks of my eggs, waiting for the real conversation to start somewhere. "Aaron's fine, man. We eat okay and he sleeps in his own room and our friend Margie watches him if we go out."

Michael waited, nodding. I realized we had the same long hair, peacenik outcasts in here.

"But Peggy's a mess," I admitted. "She wants to leave town back to Florida." He kept waiting. "We get checks on Friday, so if we go, it'll be Saturday." We'd already settled on Friday afternoon. "It may be her bullshit talkin', man. But she's pretty desperate."

He tensed his shoulders. "Panicking? Does she get hyper angry with Aaron? Shake him?" Michael knew her well.

"No, man. She usually acts good with him, just needy." I kept her lapses to myself. "She's plenty brutal with me sometimes." He showed no sympathy. "But I can deal with that."

"No, man, you can't." Michael looked around the room and then right at me. "And neither could I."

He'd given up on her when he'd brought Aaron home in the middle of the day and interrupted Peggy and me messing around. I came downstairs in a pair of his underwear that she'd thrown to me and he quickly realized why I wore them or nothing. Anyway, she came down behind me and he told her I'd be going for good. She shouted back that if so, so was she. His eyes shot bullets at us both. Through all this Aaron stood behind him, crying.

"She really is too much, man," I said. "One minute she's loving, the next some witch from hell." We'd gotten along for a few weeks

139

without any blowups until the minute Child Services knocked on the door and our peace, outside and inside the house, ended. But Michael surely understood all that. He must have been the one who sent them.

"I think you mean wraith from hell, Randy, but the 'from hell' part is what counts." He put his elbows on the table. "Maybe we can save Aaron from her together."

I said, "I guess we'd better," but I had no idea how. If someone didn't do something, we'd hit the road and eventually she'd dump me. Then what for Aaron? Sometimes when you can't see the future, it's because there's only darkness at its end.

Michael rapped his fists on the table. "I was going to buy a gun."

He watched for my reaction. I hid my disbelief behind a sip of coffee. He'd never held a gun in his life.

"But my friends went crazy and told me not to do it. They say Aaron's not my business, there's no point throwing my life away." He looked at his messy plate. "Just let things play out the way fate deals them."

I knew Michael and his buddies played cards as a risky escape from their real lives' safety. And they thought 'fate' was a concept in Greek myths. Hell, fate brought us here together. Fate is Peggy and Aaron. Fate is the up to now. What comes next is on us.

"Peggy wouldn't respect a gun," I said. "She plays every man in her life. She'd grab it, play keep-away." I wanted to keep away from Michael's shit more than Viet Nam.

Michael looked surprised I didn't react more alarmed, but he was thinking about what I said. Maybe he'd gone a little crazy like the rest of us. He took a gulp of his coffee. "Guns don't play games, Randy. I meant, kill the bitch, not threaten her." He opened his jacket. In the inside pocket—a little .22, Beretta probably, a girl's gun—the kind for shooting up close.

I swallowed hard but kept nodding. Crazier than I thought. Maybe he'd been thinking about killing me, too, but now he'd forewarned me. "Oh, man, that'd leave Aaron nowhere except some foster home or a bus to Florida." I almost reached my hands across to him. "I think she can be talked sense to, maybe if it's both of us."

He buttoned the Levi's jacket. "Psychologists say there's no such thing as reason with people like Peggy, only careful management." He sounded like a shrink. But he was a clever guy, I had to admit. He'd found a perfect, if painful, way to keep track of our drama—by making himself part of it.

The smartass in me asked, "Does psychology suggest using guns?" I had no idea what direction Michael saw this going, but no way I was throwing anyone's life away—it would really be everyone's life—giving in to such violence.

Michael smirked. "She's got the system wrapped around her little finger. Child Services gives her more chances and the courts wouldn't do a goddamned thing. I checked. We aren't related to him. All the good intentions in the world aren't going to change Peggy. She'll walk away into a new delusion if she's chased out of the old one. And now the lawyer's warned me to remove myself from the mess." His fists tightened. He was beyond his limits.

"Man, calm down. You're scaring me." I tried to look serious, since he had a hard time seeing me that way. "No shooting, Michael. Your friends are right. Get rid of the gun, take it back to the store, whatever." Michael wouldn't know how to get one illegally. "If we leave, I promise I'll keep you posted on Aaron." I tried to force his eyes on mine. "And I promise I'll stick with him."

Finally, he looked at me. "I believe you, Randy. You mean well." He gazed out the window. "All of Peggy's men mean well." He was about to cry. A very dangerous man.

After Peggy met her therapist—she never told me what happened there—and the social worker came and went, smiley as could be, we finalized our plans. I had no way to sell more dope, but we'd pick up our checks before lunchtime and those funds would get us to Florida as long as my car held up, no reason to think it wouldn't. It was one of my lucky purchases—I'd traded a mechanic a bag of pot and a couple hundred dollars for the rehabbed Gremlin hatch back. We made a list of what we needed for the trip and had a talk with Aaron about seeing Robert and Grandpa again and what he remembered about Florida—only a year gone, but to a four-year-old that's eternity.

As we packed Ari's art stuff and books, he wanted to know what would happen with Michael. Peggy yelled at him for crying and left me to calm him. I wished I could explain how Michael was as screwed up as the rest of us and how Aaron'd be okay, how everything'd be okay. But after he'd run out of tears, he clutched that damn comforter and curled into a ball on his bed. I patted his head but he said, "It's all right, Randy," like he was the parent.

On Friday, we cashed the checks and, with Aaron sad and surveilling from the back seat, drove to the Family Dollar to buy pillows and a cooler. I had a pup tent I'd been hauling around since childhood, but we'd probably just sleep in the car.

The warm day found lots of college kids around the strip mall—no classes Friday afternoons. When we pulled into the parking lot Peggy said, "All these people with no place to go. I'm glad we've got a plan." She looked into the back seat. "Mommy feels better than she has in weeks, baby. Florida will be so sunny and warm."

We went in holding hands, Aaron between us. The shopping took twenty minutes and I wheeled the cart to the car as Peggy carried Aaron like a baby, smiling as bright as I'd ever seen her and singing to him, "We're gonna fly to the sun."

We neared the hatchback and I saw Michael's van at the end of our row. He must have tailed us, and I imagined his frustration at being left out of our loop, Aaron's fucked-up family. When he'd returned Aaron on Thursday evening, and I told him we were leaving Saturday, he seemed distant and hurt more than angry, but if Peggy got into it with him now, who knew what might happen. I left the cart by my car. "Be back in a couple, Peggy," I said steadily as I could.

I heard her mutter "that sonofabitch," and Aaron let out a little gasp. I kept striding as Michael climbed down from the van. I watched his hands.

"Michael," I called out. "Hey, man, the deed's done. We're on our way outta here." I stopped a car's width away from him, in front of a worn black Mustang. I dropped my arms to my sides and opened my palms to him.

He spread his legs and took a stance. He shook his head 'no' and looked past me to Peggy and Aaron. "This will be a disaster, Randy." He fixed on me. "It's just running away. She'll never change."

I wanted to disagree but what was the point. "Man, I'll do my best, I promise."

He looked up the row of cars and his chest heaved. "That boy is so lost." His eyes dropped to the asphalt.

There was no wind left in him. I stepped forward and caught his eyes. "I'll take care of them. I will."

I looked back. Peggy scowled as she loaded the bags in the hatchback and Aaron twitched around, gazing at me and Michael with a look I can't describe. He dropped the bag he was holding, and the comforter, and bolted toward us.

Peggy shouted, "Get back here!" and glared in our direction. She picked up the bag Aaron dropped then flashed the finger as she threw it in the car. She left the blue comforter lying there.

I knelt to grab Aaron, but Michael stepped into the lane and raised his hand. He swept his head "no" even as Aaron got confused and slowed. "Ari, stop. Go to your mother."

I couldn't believe he'd given up. Peggy's smile twisted. Aaron stared wide-eyed at Michael.

"We'll meet again, Aaron. I love you." That's all Michael said.

The boy teared up, gave a little wave, and walked away.

"I promise, man. I'll watch out for him," I said. Michael's own eyes were wet. At our car, Peggy grabbed Aaron's shoulders and muttered something, shaking him a little.

Michael turned his back to them, opened his jacket, and reached in for the gun. "You take this, Randy." He looked over his shoulder at them. "I can't use it," he said, as if he actually thought I could.

I shook my head, but Michael seemed so defeated it wasn't wise to argue. "Okay, man, it'll make us safe on the road." I checked the safety and slipped the slim pistol into my jacket's inside pocket. I wished he'd given us the damned van instead.

"I'm sorry, Randy. Tell him I'm sorry." He looked at our car, but Peggy and Aaron had already loaded. He climbed into the van, revved, and pulled it into the aisle.

I walked to the car wondering what he'd have done to himself if he kept the weapon. I pulled out the key and felt the gun jab me with every movement. Michael drove by, giving one last sad look. I retrieved the comforter and made sure he saw me pass it in to Aaron. I climbed into the driver's seat but part of me wished we could all stay in town together.

Aaron knelt in the back seat, turned to the hatchback window. Peggy started up on me. "Have a good conversation with your buddy Michael?" She buckled her seat belt. "There's nothing stopping us, Randy. We'll finish packing and go." She set her jaw. "If Michael is at the house when we get there, you're both out of our lives for good." She fake-smiled at Aaron. "Isn't that right, Ari?"

I looked in the mirror. He nodded but tears were running.

"Michael won't be there, Peggy. He's out of it." But I wished that wasn't true. Now everything fell to me.

"Then let's get going."

I turned the ignition and the radio came on playing "Honky Tonk Woman." At Prospect Street I waited for traffic to pass. Aaron stood on the seat to watch for an opening. "It's just a shot away," he shouted out though it was the wrong song. He kept singing, pointing, his face red and grim. I pulled onto the street and thought maybe we'd hit McDonald's before the duplex.

I started to say something about how life goes on when Peggy burst out, "Sit down." She lashed around and slapped Aaron full-palm across his cheek. Aaron fell back and moaned.

I pulled over, the gun prodding against my ribs. Peggy twisted to hit him again. I caught her arm midswing as we came to a stop.

She scowled like she could kill me.

Aaron stared at us, open-mouthed.

Peggy jerked her arm free. "Let's just go."

Aaron covered his face with the comforter.

I forced myself back against the seat, to find control. "We'll go, Peggy, but I promise if you ever hurt him again"—I told her quiet and firm so we'd all remember to believe it—"you'll get the same from me."

————◆————

STUDENT OF THE GAME

Hiram's mother dragged him to a few Mudlarks games a year, so she could replenish the family's plastic cup supply, grab free t-shirts, maybe get a foul ball. Mom didn't have to drag his older siblings Mac or Lynzi. They loved baseball, or maybe the attention they got there. The elderly ushers were sympathetic to Mac because he was slow—okay, cognitively impaired. Lynzi scored looks from boys because she'd budded boobs last summer and since then wore tight shirts and short shorts. And the Mudlarks, single A minors, loved kids, having few players past college age themselves. They remembered the joy that brought them to the game. "Only the love can make a real ballplayer," Hiram's dad had said at the one game he'd brought them to four years ago—half Hiram's life—before he left them behind to find work in North Dakota. The bottom of the second and already the score showed Scissors 3, Mudlarks 2. The players were still learning how to play the game.

As he munched down a hotdog—it was $1 Classic Food night—Hiram guessed it wasn't so bad, yet. Mom antsied in her seat as the third Mudlark batter of the inning came to the plate.

She shouted at Gorman, who'd reached second, "C'mon home, boy." Then to Wingrove, "Bring him in, boy." Hiram wondered if she called them all "boy" because she wished Mac could play ball. Mac had tried out for Little League last year. He was old and strong enough but distracted so easily that every time up to bat he struck out, the wood still on his shoulder. Her hopes passed down to Hiram who'd try out for minor league ball next summer. His dad had given him a baseball name, Mom told him. Imagine seeing it in the program, the announcer intoning—Hiram McGinty. "Hit 'em, Hiram!" or "Hoist a high one, Hiram." Even "Murder it, McGinty." But when Mom suggested that one she teared up, probably thinking of poor Mac or his disappeared dad.

The giveaways began before the third inning. Mom had it all figured out. Go early on a night some local company offered free tickets, and find seats close to the field just past the home team dugout. There you could chat up ball boys, assistant managers, and the older kids hired to toss prizes and conduct contests between innings. Later in the season, free nights would be packed, but tonight, only two weeks in, the bleachers down the lines were empty, and closer in, maybe a third of the newer fold-down seats held beer-swilling old-timers in beat-up Brewers, Twins, or Cardinals caps, young couples here for a cheap date, or overweight women and their kids, usually in packs of at least three, like his family.

Sure enough, when Wingrove struck out swinging it didn't take ten seconds before the recorded organ sounded a fanfare and the announcer proclaimed, "Coming Your Way, Mudlarks T-Shirts, Thanks to Pansky Chevrolet!" Hiram's Mom jumped up, tossing her arms so wildly she looked like a giant octopus. The girl tossing the shirts looked past her and lobbed the knotted fabric six rows behind them where two older boys with ball gloves waved like they knew her. His mom cast an evil eye on the girl. "The fix is in," she said loud enough the girl stared then threw another shirt so hard it got past Mom's flaying arms and caught her in the chest. She "umphed" sitting, untying the shirt. As always, the Mudlarks logo sat high on the chest while the auto-dealer's name shouted on the back. He'd be wearing t-shirts like that all summer, new ones or stretched-out hand-me-downs from Mac or Lynzi.

Mac crossed the aisle to sit by himself. The usher dramatically dusted his seat and called Mac "sir" before Mac started shucking peanuts. Mom smiled at Hiram and put the shirt in the bag she brought to carry their trophies home. He noted "t-shirt" at the bottom of the scorecard he'd sketched out at home. As the Mudlarks took the field Lynzi stood, looked up at the older boys and applauded, bouncing. One boy elbowed the other until Mom caught on and pulled Lynzi by the shirttails. Hiram wished his dad had left advice about girls.

Top of the third passed with one Scissors' hit that should have been an error on shortstop Gonzalez, but hometown players usually escaped the penalty. The "Smile Cam" sponsored by Dr. Jordan's Dental killed time while the Mudlarks prepared to bat. In center field the electronic scoreboard, the only fancy thing in the old park, showed closeups of fans who were supposed to show their teeth. Last year the camera had caught their family as Hiram reviewed his scorekeeping. Mom poked him until he looked up to see her and his siblings grinning like chimps. The camera moved before he could smile and Mom complained about his "bad attitude." This time he kept his eye on the screen but the camera didn't choose them.

All three Mudlarks fanned in the bottom of the third and Hiram put a star next to the Scissors' pitcher's name—Sebastiano Bonaparte. Now there was a baseball name! "Beat 'em down, Bonaparte," "Bean him, 'Bastiano!" He was a Haitian from Florida. Hiram understood only that Haiti was an island where disasters happened and they spoke French. Bonaparte he recognized as the old general guy. Hiram wished his name was exotic and not barn-yard hick. He wished he was from some foreign country, disasters or not. But being here seemed disaster enough. Mac threw a peanut at him and in doing so spilled his own huge Mountain Dew. Mom rushed over to clean Mac up, scowling—at Hiram. Mac laughed when she swiped at him with one of the towelettes she carried in the bag. Mac made a mess at least hourly.

Out in right field three fans, each one half of a coupled team, put on hip waders, fake beards, and railroad-style caps. The um-pire blew her whistle and the competitors pushed blow-up beer barrels every which way to their partners. Then the first teammate stripped off the costume and the second clumsily dressed over their street clothes. They'd picked the teams earlier at the turn-stiles. Hiram was glad he'd never be picked. He and clumsy Mac, or he and snarky Lynzi, or, even worse, he and blubbery, bluster-ing Mom. The second rollers wrestled the barrels to the foul line where the umpire declared a winner. Team mascot Muddy, who looked pretty much like a giant piece of poop with a beak peeking out under a Mudlarks cap, patted everyone's back. Some crowd members close to the action clapped, but many found the pause a good time to go get beer. The announcer suggested, "Your local lager, handcrafted by the good folks at Sky King Brewery," which had of course sponsored the drunken-looking race. Hiram shook his head and noted "beer race" on his card. Mom returned to her seat and bumped his arm, causing his pencil to make a wavy line he'd have to deal with at home since the miniature golf pencil he brought had no eraser.

The fourth inning passed. Two Scissors runs made it 5-2. Mudlarks player Howie Huffman—hardly a real sports name—answered three questions on the screen: who's your favorite, Fallon or Conan? Jetsons or Flintstones? Katniss or Daenerys? Then, after banging two balls to deep left but foul, Huffman struck out. Hiram's chest sank. On most fouls hit their way he was ready to drop the scorecard and grab his glove. But if the ball came off the bat at all hard, he ducked though against his will. Mac never flinched, Mom had noted more than once, even though Mac's glove rarely left the concrete, his hands typically full of food.

Between innings the promo girls underhanded Softee balls to lucky fans. Mom pointed eagerly at Hiram and Lynzi. His sister looked away, using the shame as an excuse to check out the boys again. She hadn't checked her phone even once. Hiram put down his scorecard and stood with his glove. He tried to appear needy but when it looked like the girl would pass them by, he waved his gloved hand and jumped up and down like Mom taught him. The girl tossed a ball so he had to lurch for it. His elbow banged on Lynzi's seat as he shoved her aside to make the catch. But he got the ball and the ball girl grinned. Not Lynzi—she batted at him as if he was an insect. "You brat." She pouted when she saw the boys laughing.

Mom said, "Oh, you got one, Hiram, good catch," far more excited than he was. He showed her the ball, branded with the Mudlarks logo and an ad for Mr. Softee ice cream, but before he could show Mac, Mom grabbed the ball and shoved it in their bag.

Midway through the fifth, the pizza giveaway seemed wasted on $1 food night. But a fan above the first base dugout acted thrilled when the delivery girl—they changed shirts for different products—helped him open the box, big-screen camera focused on the cheesy pie. Time for his second hot dog, Hiram hoped. Mom said yes and made Lynzi take him up to the food stalls, also to get her another Diet Pepsi and Mac a Mountain Dew. And don't forget popcorn.

Hiram flew up the steps, but Lynzi did a kind of catty slink, touching seatbacks with slow-motion fingers, her eyes returning to the guys. One of them winked and the other made a grabbing gesture with his gloved hand. Hiram waited for her to catch up, but fixed on the dudes so they'd know he was watching.

But when they reached the food stand, Lynzi hit him hard on the arm. "Seriously, Hiram, stay out of my life or I will kill you."

She ordered, adding cheese nachos for herself and forgetting his hot dog until he spoke up. "Remember that's we came up here for in the first place, not your stupid boys."

"Mom sent us up here so she'd get a break from you, weirdo." Lynzi nudged him and ordered three dogs. "When Mom sees yours, she'll want one, but first she'll say 'no, I'm watching my weight.' And Mac will drool." She balanced the drinks and two popcorns in a corrugated tray and left Hiram to apply mustard and relish at the condiments cart.

At the stairs Lynzi leaned against the railing. But instead of older boys, a man in a black and white striped shirt came up to talk to her. She blushed and shook her head no, but the man kept talking. Hiram stuffed the last dog into its warming bag and rushed over.

"C'mon, honey, you'll have fun," the man said.

Up close Hiram saw he was probably just past high school age, same as the players. The shirt made him look important. "Leave her alone. She's my sister." Hiram tried to sound tough, hard to do holding three hot dogs. Lynzi looked at him like he was crazy.

"No, kid." The guy chuckled. "I want your family to run in the sack relay after next inning, the three of you."

"The other team they'd picked left early," Lynzi explained. Hiram's dad always told him the game wasn't over 'til it was over.

"You mean, and Mom?" Mom would kill them before they'd get her on the field.

Lynzi frowned. "No, us and Mac, dummy."

The man again said, "C'mon, you kids'll have fun, I promise."

Lynzi looked at the boys a few rows above. They were following her actions. "You in, Hiram?" she asked.

"Okay, I guess. Mac will like it." And Mom will like the prizes, Hiram thought. Really, he wasn't so sure about Mac.

The fifth had ended and the Mudlarks were back on the field. Somehow, they'd gotten a run. A double and a single, Mom reported. 5-3. But she'd been ignored during the ballcap giveaway, sorry. She waved off the hot dog then relented when Mac unwrapped his and Lynzi munched her nachos. Hiram told Mom about the race and she sputtered she was proud they'd been picked, though they hadn't won anything yet.

The Scissors sent six to the plate, left two on base, went up 6-3. The game slowed and Hiram wondered about the race. Which of them should go first, who should finish? Lynzi wasn't weighted down by her new body, so she'd run lead-off, maybe even distract the other team if they were older boys. Then Mac, if he'd run when Lynzi tagged him. Hiram would bat cleanup, make Mom proud when he brought them home winners.

The big screen came on and the "Dance Cam" panned the picnic seats outside left field. Kids threw themselves around like maniacs. Mac danced wildly. He tried to pull Lynzi up with him but she said it was time for them to go to the gate by the bullpen. Mac bragged on how fast he'd run—maybe a hundred miles an hour! Lynzi acted motherly with Mac, steering with hands on his shoulders. But she checked to make sure the boys were following. Hiram felt like he was on the bench, separate from all of them. The promotions guy gave them the rundown on rules, looking at Hiram and his brother as if they were twins in slowness, both carrying gloves useless for the contest.

Meanwhile, after two outs the Mudlarks put men on first and second, double and an intentional walk. If Hiram had still been closely keeping score—Mom held his card—the game would seem even more exciting. Tying run Huffman stood at the plate. He took a good cut but missed an inside fastball. The pitcher, still Bonaparte throwing fire, caught the outside corner with a curve. Huffman lumbered to the plate again, looked serious, and blooped a foul their way. Hiram got his glove up but the ball caught the thumb and bounced onto the field. Mac went wide-eyed and Lynzi gasped loud enough their mother must have heard. Reserve player number 27 picked up the ball and Hiram opened the mitt wide for the gift. But the player said, "One out per batter, son." He underhanded the ball gently enough even Mac couldn't miss it. Mac's face lit up and Lynzi urged him to raise the ball for all to see. Mom was clapping and signaled for Mac to bring the ball to her, but too late. Huffman fanned again and the promo guy opened the gate and led them onto the field.

Hiram and Mac turned over their gloves. The field squished under his feet like new sneakers. The announcer went on about "beans from around the world" as the umpire girl handed out scratchy sacks printed with steaming coffee cups. They positioned the teams along the foul stripe from the dirt behind third halfway to the warning track. Lynzi helped Mac step into his sack before she went furthest out. The members of the other team—the Snethens, what kind of name was that?—were older, but lined up so Lynzi would go first against the littlest, maybe Mac's age, ten. In the middle Mac would race a chubby girl about Lynzi's twelve. This left Hiram against a boy old enough to be a freshman. It didn't seem fair, but maybe the dropped ball still stung his spirit. No one's a failure until they stop trying, his dad told him.

Hiram looked at the TV screen Mac refused give up the foul ball even though it made him strain to hold the sack. The announcer sang, "Filbert's Coffee Makes You Ready ... Set ... Go!" Lynzi covered her ten yards in smooth leaps, building a good lead. She tagged Mac but it took a push in the right direction for him to struggle away. He got halfway to Hiram before he dropped the baseball and hopped more properly. The ball rolled toward Hiram, distracting the Snethen girl so she stumbled. At least he'd have the chance to go down swinging.

Hiram leaned and retrieved the rolling ball then reached out to receive Mac's tag. Instead, Mac dodged Hiram, cried out "I'm safe" and headed into left field. Lynzi darted after Mac. Hiram was more concerned when the racing girl tagged her brother. Thankfully the bigger boy paid more attention to Mac's whooping—he ran in circles while Lynzi chased him—than his leg of the race. Hiram knew Mac hadn't really tagged him but surely close enough. He took off hopping, holding the ball—*our* ball—against his stomach along with the sack's stiff edge. The older boy made up ground but Hiram high-fived the umpire first.

Lynzi led Mac over to where the promo guy and umpire conferred. The announcer stayed quiet. The Snethen kids pointed along the foul line—then at the McGintys. Hiram felt guilty, a little, that he'd fudged the tag. "Do we have a winner?" the metallic voice finally asked. But a picture of the Mudlarks relief pitcher replaced the camera view of their contest. "Let's hear it for all the kids," the announcer intoned as the umpire raised the big Snethen boy's hand into the air and presented Lynzi some coupons. It was only a game, his dad would say, but it meant more than a game. Mac grabbed the baseball from Hiram and stuck out his tongue. Nothing was going Hiram's way.

They settled again and Mom collected the foul ball—"You write down who hit it, Hiram"—and the coffee coupons, and put them in the bag. She rustled Mac's bristly hair and tried to stroke the green streak in Lynzi's messy locks. She patted Hiram on the shoulder. "You're all winners to me." Nearby fans applauded them.

Hiram grumped through the Scissors' quick seventh, stood still during the pause while Mac sang "Take Me Out to the Ballgame" and Lynzi stretched to the point of bursting though the older boys ignored her. Mom struggled to her feet but smiled when she caught Hiram looking. He wanted to apologize for dropping the foul, for trying to cheat. He wished he'd won something worth winning, but still they made a good haul, didn't they?

The Mudlarks got back another run in the seventh, now 5-4, and Hiram returned to his scorekeeping as they tossed leftover t-shirts before the eighth. The relief pitcher, Geoff Antle—good name, Mom whispered—let the Scissors hit his sliders and cut them down on three soft ground balls. Lots of ways to get an out, he remembered his dad saying.

The older boys left with nary a wink and Lynzi glowered next to Mac, finishing their popcorn. Mom let out a snore even as the screen came on and the announcer shouted, "Beware the Infamous Kiss Cam!" Hiram wondered why this late game entertainment had no sponsor—maybe love didn't need one?

A young couple sharing a blanket in left field startled as they recognized themselves and laid big smackers on each other. What would Lynzi have done with those older boys if she hadn't run the sack race instead of more flirting?

The camera jerked along the foul line and caught the ball girl chatting up player #27. They pulled apart and the thinner crowd catcalled and booed because they didn't kiss.

Then Hiram was there on the screen, holding his stupid score-card next to his drowsy mother whose eyes opened wide when

Lynzi shouted, "Mom!" She looked heavy and worn and he suddenly feared the people's laughter might aim at her. He remembered his parents kissing, and one more thing his dad had said at their game together.

Hiram dropped his scorecard, put his hand on his mother's shoulder, and puckered up. Some guy called, "Hey, kid, you dropped something," but Mom kissed so gently it felt like a tear falling on his lips. The crowd applauded and cheered, even Lynzi and Mac. He heard his dad say, "That's right, Hiram, it's how you play the game."

———•———

THE CARDSELLERS

MOST OF THE PUBLISHERS' REPRESENTATIVES IN L.A were fifty-year-old suburban sharpies in powder-blue leisure suits with flowered shirts unbuttoned to where their stomachs puffed like tanned dough rising from too-tight pans. Our little literary bookstore didn't stock the bestsellers—we three partners were the noble sort. Near impossible to get any of those guys to spend an afternoon taking our single-copy orders for fifty backlist paperbacks and ten of whatever one serious novel the big publisher was risking a loss on that quarter. Getting the reps to talk to would-be writers in faded jeans and "Hank Chinaski" teeshirts for a measly fifty bucks commission was, shall we say, at *their* convenience.

But they didn't intimidate us. I mean, nobility and all should rise, and these folks thought that Anne Rice was a "southern writer" like Flannery O'Connor. Their attempts to drop names in some backhanded compliment to our literary—if not retailing—competence made them seem all the worse to me. And their endless drive for "success" made me worry all the more about the several past noble failures—money, women, family—that pressed at my memory.

But Roger Hawkins had come into the store about a week after we'd opened, responding to a month's old request we'd made to Blue Starling Press up in Santa Bonita to place an order for their important line of contemporary-classic poetry. Roger showed up in his plaid slacks and one of those 'alligator' pullovers, a little younger and a bit less chubby and a little more easygoing than the rest.

He proceeded to write up our order for ten copies of the entire backlist and twenty for every new title. His facial twitching showed me that he thought we were as crazy as hell, but after a few bewildered sighs, Roger got into the swing of things. "Okay," he said, "okay, hey, you guys are going places with this store, I can feel it." His choice to go with the absurd seemed a good sign. "Really, good vibes in here. Nice shelves." Well, we had done the store in native redwood and built everything ourselves.

Roger then packed up his order forms and started for the door. He'd just made some quick and unexpected bucks. We'd already started grinning behind his back when he popped back around and stood like he wanted a fight. "Are you guys nuts? Who in hell are you gonna sell this stuff to?"

Those happened to be two of our favorite questions—we at least got to speak up about noble causes—and Roger ended up sticking around for two hours and a few beers, and even missed an appointment at Harrier's Books in Bountiful Hills (who, Roger laughed, owed every publisher big money). All this before he got around to trying to sell us anything else.

Which was *cards*! Windmill Cards, with Huntervasser and Klimt, super-realism from the Southern California School, and turn-of-the-century illustrations of Shakespeare, Andersen, and brothers Grimm. It was a new card company, different. Roger carried a lot of stuff from small operations, being a hustler of a unique kind—like we thought of ourselves.

We weren't interested in cards, we told him, having vowed to one another no escapes—no cards, no calendars, no Harlequin and nothing written or ever to be written by Erich Segal, Arthur Hailey, Jackie Susann, or by that unmentionable raspy-voiced "poet" who wrote: "the thunder is God's trombones."

Roger encouraged us to "compromise," if only to "save this grand experiment," as he began to call it. "At least take the cards," he begged. "I personally guarantee you they'll sell here, and you got to admit they're pretty as hell."

Well…we did take the cards—escapist stuff—and I even began using them for every thin piece of correspondence I mustered to distant relatives and old friends who only seemed older as we three became nobler, and poorer, and lonelier. The beautiful cards made you want to write something happy just to be able to send them. And Roger was indeed right: we sold them—unlike our favorite books of poetry and new fiction—by the dozen.

But, of course, back on that first day we met him, Roger, after prying open our empty vaults moving us into the card business, tried to get us to "take a few of these Froggy Friends," too, for the kids." We passed and Roger parted that day with a forgiving smile than understood next-to-nothing about us.

Roger hustled for the little guys, it turned out, and worked his tail off for us, smallest of the small. Our Blue Starling order had been the biggest he'd ever filed with them, and it apparently earned him some special treatment. He came in one day, offering to arrange an exclusive signing party for Hank Chinaski's new book for fall, a literary moment for a Los Angeles bookstore akin to Hemingway showing up to toast your new manuscript and bringing along Maxwell Perkins to do the editing.

Roger understood by then that we'd be mildly excited, if also terrified at the possibilities for disaster. Chinaski, after all, made no bones about his distaste for literary happenings. And he was well known for remaining for weeks on antagonistic benders. But Roger was perhaps the most excited of all—the signing would "make the store." And so, with our dubious approval, Roger went off with the mission to get a clearer idea about possible dates.

The signing party work brought us closer. Roger, I learned, had two great passions. The L.A. Dodgers—which was perfectly horrible if, like me, you're a Reds fan. And, his mother. They had season tickets at Dodger Stadium. They also traveled around the West together. Roger was always talking about some outing to Napa, Santa Fe, even Tijuana. And Roger still lived at the family homestead in the Valley. With Mom.

I thought it strange that a semi-normal guy like Roger still spent so much time with his mother, who would have to have been at least sixty, even giving balding, pudgy Roger the benefit of the doubt. But we got along because of the baseball, and I figured that his dealings with his mother might be seen by some as touching, as opposed to weird. It might only be that he hadn't worked up a solid sense of self, which, when I thought about it in terms of my own noble example, might have been the wiser choice.

Anyway, Roger and I got along, and I occasionally sent him a card to ask about Chinaski and to rib him about the Dodgers. I'd get back one of the Froggy Friends with some message like "Cinci Reds, boo, boo, boo, all I want is Dodger Blue... and I got Chinaski all for you." A self-satisfied amphibian grinned on the card's cover.

Blue Starling finally confirmed the date for Chinaski's signing, and we ordered one hundred fifty hardcovers and three hundred fifty paperbacks of *Riding the Bulldog Home, While Singing Aunt Jemima*—or something like that. We decided to bypass any problems of riot at the signing by just flowing with it, Southern California style, and so planned to order two kegs of lager and, depending on how much business we'd done any particular day, from two bottles to two cases of Stoli, Chinaski's preferred beer chaser. Jack, most timid of us partners, wanted to hire security guards, but we decided that based on most guards we'd ever seen they'd likely be as drunk as the poet and not half as mean.

Roger tried to salve our fears. "I'll be there to watch him. I've met the man. He's no ogre. He's a lot like you guys: he just likes to drink a lot and talk big." And, Roger might have added that both we and Chinaski often got ourselves into more trouble than we could handle.

But our favorite rep made the arrangements and things went well with the party still a month down the road. We expected to make about $3,000 on the day, a lot of money for a store averaging about $250 a day gross, not to mention the free advertising.

Then Chinaski got sick, or just balked, and the book printing was fouled up, and Roger left town during the hiatus, with his mother, to see the Grand Canyon. I expected to get some Froggy Friend saying something like "this pit's as deep as the one the Reds are digging themselves into behind the Blue." Something clever I had no mood for.

But when we didn't hear anything from anyone for two weeks, I called Blue Starling to check on Chinaski and mentioned Roger's name.

Their secretary informed me: "I'm sorry, but Mr. Hawkins died last week. He fell into the Grand Canyon."

I said "what?" and she repeated, "he fell into the Grand Canyon," in a peevish tone.

I checked the previous week's obits, feeling too distant to call Roger's mother for details, and found the four-line listing everyone not in the movie business gets in the L.A. papers. The obit listed accidental death in Grand Canyon National Park, Arizona.

It ended up that the Chinaski deal fell through due to the man's changeable temperament. Blue Starling told me he wasn't going to do the signing anywhere else, either, and that Roger the order Roger must have upped the order: two hundred hardcovers and five hundred paperbacks of Chinaski's new book.

Several weeks passed and we went ahead and coughed up a lot fewer copies, one keg of beer and some cheap wine, and staged a "No Chinaski Signing Party" that drew about six people besides acquaintances who'd heard about the free booze. Somebody that day even walked out with the single copy we'd stocked of some university press's collection of Arabic poetry which, at $40 paper, had turned out to be printed only in Arabic! We'd gotten good at taking punches and pretending to roll with them. We read our own poetry and drank a round for Roger, but by this time the cryptic "he fell into the Grand Canyon" had become an old joke. Even I laughed, if with tinges of both bitterness and shame.

A few days later, I was working the counter when a frail lady about seventy creaked in with a cane and another old woman of much greater bulk. In their mismatched print dresses they looked like a Fellini version of Laurel and Hardy. But they shuffled their way to the counter.

"Can I help you ladies?" I asked, expecting some request for the latest issue of *Cat Fancier's Digest,* or, if it were to be a lucky day, perhaps an illustrated Shakespeare.

"Are you Steve?" The thin woman's voice crackled like a gramophone.

"Yes?" I asked, putting nothing together, too amused with my inner sarcasm.

"Roger told me all about your store." I got nervous, then almost chuckled, thinking about 'Grand Canyon' and what I'd found odd about their relationship. "Roger said it was one of the nicest stores. And I can see he was right."

"Well, thank you, ma'am." I fell back on my Midwestern twang, but my voice fluttered. I wanted to ask about Roger's mishap, but also for the uncomfortable situation to be over.

"He was very fond of you all, you know. Especially you, Steve.

Such good young men, struggling for your own ideals with books."
She sounded like everybody's grandmother. "Like Roger," she continued, her eyes suddenly farther away, blinking to stay ahead of
tears.

"Roger was a good guy," I mumbled, then said something about
not hearing about the accident in time to make the funeral.

"Oh, you heard from one of his other friends," she said without
question. "It was awful. He was taking photographs for our travel
album, leaning out over a railing. I got dizzy watching. Then he
leaned too far." Now she began shaking. I did too. The other lady
shook her head at me in a tragic aside. The cliché about great blow
to all came to mind. The big woman took Roger's mother's arm
and guided her from the counter.

I said, "I'm really sorry, Mrs. Hawkins. I miss him, too. Roger
was a real nice guy."

Roger's mother stopped at the end of the counter. "We must
buy something, Mary."

And she glanced over the row of unsold Chinaski faces in
our "bestseller" section, then found what she wanted. She picked
through the rack of Windmill Cards, then tottered to me, smiled,
and laid out two dollars for the pretty card illustrating Andersen,
with the fairy princess Thumbelina reaching out to her friend the
butterfly.

TRACKING NEAL

DEAN AND I COME BACK DRUNK TO my place in San Miguel I've shared with him since he arrived a week ago, unannounced. His backpack sits near the table with the rickety wicker chairs where my laptop looms, unused as a rusted typewriter. We're getting nothing done but drinking, singing "La Adelita" as we wander the cobblestone streets like resurrected ghosts. I must help him remember the words we learned twenty years ago when we trekked Mexico together on my college graduation trip. Dean's energy convinced me our wandering ways would never change, but I've moved on. And our vague romance seems unrecoverable as he still believes his own motion—forward, backward, sideways—must remain constant. When I complain that he distracts my work, Dean says, "You remember how to do it, man—just write."

My name's John Little, like Robin Hood's sidekick, and you can guess what Dean calls me, but he's the one more likely to borrow from the rich. Despite my dumpy lair he thinks I have money. There is my mother's dependable funding and my inclination for steady if poorly paying work. My stories—travel escapades for wannabes—do sell. So to Dean I'm a success, a man of means.

And Dean's the continent's most endearing freeloader.

He's come down to Old Mexico to search out the death place of Neal Cassady, aka Dean Moriarty in Jack Kerouac's *On the Road*, for whom his hippie parents named him, perhaps setting in motion some vagabond curse. Dean will finish up his 42nd year next week and seems to think his time is running out since Neal died on railroad tracks here a few days before he reached that age. Dean's loved such synchronicity since our youth, made myths of the trouble he's found while chasing his visions, the adventures he's drug me into.

I love him still, even though I've gone loner and he's far worse for wear. In this cheap room of adobe walls, ancient furniture, and ceiling fan that sputters, I open my arms and he falls into me smelling of tequila and lime. Our collective weight drags us to the narrow bed where in a second he's asleep in his t-shirt and jeans. I pull off his boots then nestle in beside him.

Oh, this life. I awake to Dean's heavy breathing. This morning—sunshine flooding through the festive curtains. This love—despite absences of weeks, years. Between the two of us five marriages, ended now. Or rather my two ended; Dean's three are over but incomplete. To Stella he sends child support. His Amy sends pleading letters. Sharon, his young bride only five years ago, do-nates just-passing-through sex and checks, unwittingly covering the child support to Stella. This messy life of his again vexes mine.

Climbing out of bed I scrape my thigh on the wooden frame. Dean grins though his face has narrowed, stubble gone gray, eyes crow's-footed. Today we'll search out Neal's train tracks. Despite devout seekers across the years, nothing in San Miguel marks his death, or life, here. Dean wants to place a plaque at his lodging at Beneficenia #17 or his favorite bar, La Cucaracha (long moved from the Plaza Principal), or at least to plant a message of remembrance by the rails in the high desert if we can find the fatal spot.

I scratch up fried eggs on tortillas and beans, a fresh orange for each of us. Several days ago we bought lunch for Harvey, *un gringo viejo* Dean found who claimed to have known Neal here back in '68. Harv had been a young man with many friends then, studying art at the famous Instituto, adventuring like the Beats, escaping the 'Nam draft hiding out like Butch or Sundance in hovels, bodegas, and whorehouses. The stuff of legends. He'd never returned home to Cleveland and now no one, there or here, cares for him. "A hanger-on, to place and past," Dean commiserated after we'd nodded belief at Harv's stories, bought his *comida*, Dos Equis, and shots, then left the old guy in the afternoon shadows with two hundred pesos for his trials and trouble. "Sad, man," Dean said, but I couldn't help but see my friend in the geezer's gauzy gaze.

On ensuing days, local denizens repeated details of Neal's sad ending, in either hospital or post office, having been hauled inside, comatose from drugs, drink, or the cold. We'll search tonight for the last witness on Dean's list—Witt, who wears a pork-pie hat and haunts the classier cantinas. He'd famously invited Neal to a wedding party the night of his demise.

Despite Dean's suggestion otherwise, we take our morning showers separately. Our trek to the train station has been postponed too long by hangovers or distractions, and I make the coffee strong with purpose. Dean comes out dripping wet, toweling his crew cut hair. He lifts a leg onto a chair and dries the thigh, knee, calf, ankle, foot, every move seeming to pose for me. He knows he's been my model, not just for characters in my stories, but for the wandering chapters of my real life. Don't we all see our friends' mistakes clearly and excuse our own as imitations? And hasn't he mimicked me in his stable times, attempting marriage, channeling aimlessness into writing? I help him dry his back, and he murmurs, "Old friend, I thank you" and tries to kiss me. I let him, hold his body until the moment stills, both of us silent in forgiveness.

The sun shreds high clouds into banners, welcomes us outside. San Miguel's classically Mexican historic district holds distinction as a World Heritage Site, her downtown absent of fast food and neon, her streets still cobblestone. But the sidewalks allow smooth walking and we clip downhill like younger men chasing dreams. Dean laughs even when he begins coughing as our walk turns into race near El Jardín, the local *plaza principal*. The fabled pink cathedral La Parroquía gleams like a gothic Gaudí in the sun. Tourists gawk at the fluid spires and distorted angles, but frown at our lack of decorum in a place so spiritually packaged. Dean looks like a cowboy in his boots, jeans, and t-shirt under an open jacket, same outfit he's worn since college. I'm in shorts, sandals, pullover. "You've gone yuppie," he accuses, though he's regretted the jeans and jacket in every afternoon's heat. Still he wears his traditions like a badge despite his claims of constant reinvention.

In the *zócalo*, we choose a wrought iron bench and sit. Dean's winded. Across the green near the bandstand, a clown juggles fake bowling pins, drops them, turns a cartwheel, grins mea culpa. Several children applaud, giggling wide-eyed. Dean rises, his hands juggling invisible objects. When he drops them, his own cartwheel lands him butt up on the lawn. The father of a passing Mexican family laughs while his wife scurries her children away from *el gringo loco*. Dean brushes himself off and bows. Even the mother smiles as the family moves on, kids waving to my friend.

Dean collapses back onto the bench. He tires easily. Face thinned, pores enlarged, he looks older than me though I top him by a full year. Somehow it hurts more to think of him aging than think myself old. I jot this thought in the notebook I carry. Usually, we move too fast to scribble. As he watches me write, Dean's eyes betray his loss of inspiration. I click my pen, pull him to his feet. "Times-a-wastin', pardner," I joke. "On the road, my good man."

My shtick cheers Dean up and we toss some coins into the real clown's flowery hat. They clink amid a good haul and we smile at each other, clown and Dean and me—fellow travelers.

Then it's up Calle Insurgentes for a nip at the Cantina La Colonia. New word from our scouts has Witt at the Berlin Bar tonight, a Thursday. The route through the storytellers is more circuitous than the route to the station, down by the arroyo, which is no longer the outskirts of town. San Miguel spreads in neighborhoods that become condo communities away from the center. Despite the steep slopes, this is high desert, countryside possessed by scraggly trees, scrub bushes, and random grasses. Color strikes when sun glints through thin clouds. At the right time of year, not now, the dry earth blooms white with mesquite and yucca for a few days, then settles back into peaceful earthen browns.

Dean's more interested in the architecture, Spanish colonial stone and adobe painted in native patterns. Green, red, and white mix from flags to mailboxes—fiesta everywhere. Several blocks downhill, artisan shops—weavers of rugs, bakers of ceramics, workers of wood—mix with appliance repairmen, watch-fixers, and cobblers boasting 10,000 pairs of *huaraches*. Finally the streets broaden into a suburban sprawl of fast food, Pemex stations, flea markets, and one-a-block Oxxo convenience stores. Dean asks if there's a bull ring, but it's long gone, too uncivilized for the gringo taste that steers the town. When we stop to catch our breath, Dean coughs again and I scan the cityscape towering above us. Highest up, mansions of expat retirees and artistes of inherited indulgence create a jagged castle of battlements and turrets. Would Neal and his fellow Beats bother to stop in a place so tainted?

We push on to the station—desolate yellow stone with iron-barred windows atop a foundation of crumbling concrete. Rusted metal signs direct to ticketing and information. A newer red-painted one warns: "*Peligro—Cerrado al Público.*" Nothing's ever been closed to Dean and he scrambles onto the platform, wipes at a window's grunge, succeeds only in soiling his jacket's sleeve. "This is the dust Neal Cassady choked on, LJ. Thick as a grave is deep."

He smirks at his somber thought, wanting me to argue him out of darkness. He raps the window and I stiffen with fear he'll eviscerate himself on the shards as he climbs through, bleed out on the gray concrete with only me as witness.

Last night at El Gato Negro he was loudly insistent. "You have to write it, Little John, the Dean story. Whatever this searching is. Use me, man. Make me your vessel." He tossed back a shot of tequila and called for more. But Mexico is no backdrop for American westerns anymore, its romance faded. Even swinging-door cantinas expect civility. The barkeep scowled and turned us out. As we staggered uphill Dean told me, "My whole life, always getting booted. Maybe that's why I take off first." I protested, but Dean's face projected no remorse. His lost soul his own choosing. And me, chosen apostle to his constant escape.

On the platform Dean rattles a door that shrieks like the forlorn whistle of a train. If one appeared, Dean would board it, shrug and wave from the caboose, disappear in smoke and roar. He poses on the concrete's edge. "Come up here with me, Little John."

I shake my head and scan the tracks' long descent into the scrub and desert south toward Celaya, the direction of Neal's death march. How many times has Dean left me to chase his phantom self after tormenting me with my own? He leaps and tries to wrestle me to the dust, chuckling and snorting. I remember his arms as stronger, my own legs more willing to give. It's no great effort to stand my ground until he stops and hangs around my neck like a panting boy. "Let's walk just a mile," he begs. "We'll see a sign. I'll know it."

But I know that if he doesn't sense the spot, he'll follow Neal to doom. I say, "Maybe tomorrow. Let's see what Witt tells us." I head back uphill and Dean follows, his eyes flitting for distractions. Quiet like this, he drifts past conflict, becomes his own island, protected by the sea around him from reality. If I don't reach across it, tomorrow he'll be gone.

We check in at La Cuacaracha, but no leads. Witt eats around seven in various places, leaving himself plenty of time to hit upscale cantinas for hours of drinks and talk. We leave after one tequila shot. Dean's t-shirt is sweated through as he yawns in the thin mountain air.

Back at the apartment, he collapses onto the bed, his claimed territory, and I use his bedroll for a pillow on the floor, watching the ceiling fan's monotonous rotation.

An hour later, water's running and Dean's tenor belts out "Guantanamera," the romantic Cuban anthem. Maybe next, he'll be a revolutionary there. Fine with me, my sore back says.

Dean dries himself on the balcony, his nakedness alit in the red sunset. By the time I shower and dress, he's chattering about how finding Witt will make him feel closer to Neal's story. "Then, *mi amigo*," he says, "back on the road." He raises his eyebrows—will I leave with him? A cooling shadow crosses the blazing sunset. Volcanic ash rising from Mexico City? Lights scattered from Guadalajara? No, too far from either city. Is it only me who sees red?

Dean paces around me then stands bare foot against my sandal as we admire the sky's glory. He asks directly, "Will you come with me?"

I avoid his question. "Why do you so like standing naked in the public air?"

Dean pulls away in fake shock. "Naked? Man, the skin is the thickest thing we wear." His eyes narrow. "Flesh isn't transparent. It's fabric you can't change out of." I glance toward the table and my notebook. "You can wash it, you can oil it, you can tan it, but it's your own special skin drying out and shriveling. Tightens around you, man, like a shroud."

He puts on fresh jeans and the only button-up he's brought, broad blue stripes, as dressed to kill as Dean comes. I know he wants to leave town with a bang.

At the Posada San Francisco's courtyard restaurant, Julian's, we sit under bougainvillea and greet incoming diners with *¡buen provecho!* I order us bon voyage filets, béarnaise for Dean, Bordelaise for me. It's my favorite place in town, pricey but *riquísimo*.

The old guitarist, Teodoro, takes a seat on a wobbly chair and tunes. He gauges the crowd and melodramatically strums "El Rey." He winks at me, the song pure pop. Tourists place chins in hands and Teddy hams it up. His foot pounds out time as he turns the song into Mexican martial music, missing only trumpets' blare.

Dean can't resist drumming the glass-topped table. I feel like a native surrounded by false visions, forced to play along. Dean hasn't found Neal but maybe he feels like he's again found me. I'm glad he visited. Even though I'd like him to leave, but leave happy.

We finish our steaks, a bottle of wine. Teodoro thanks me for the drink I sent him. I introduce Dean, *mi amigo para toda la vida*, my friend for life. Teddy smiles crookedly and takes Dean's hand. "*Mis amigos*, now 'La Adelita' for the two of you."

About once a week I come here, request Pancho Villa's marching song about pursuing the elusive soldier-woman. Teodoro's version replaces the quick-step march with romance, lilting, forlorn, his rough voice the wounded soldier's. *Y si Adelita se fuera con otro, la seguiría por tierra y por mar.* If Adelita leaves with another, I'd follow her by land and sea. Chatter ceases. I fell in love with this song on our driving trip through Mexico. Here at Julian's when I first asked for it, Teodoro's smile told me I'd made a friend because I knew the classic tune, the noble bandido's myth. Young musicians often don't, or play it as corny history, revolution out of style.

I wonder if Dean remembers it. His hand taps time near mine—he's getting antsy. I close my eyes and march inside my head with the music, my real life here in San Miguel my escape.

Back on the street, Dean's ramped up, glancing from the bright *zócalo* up narrow streets shadowed under the church's pink spires' spotlights. We pass banks, then a modern *hamburguesas* joint where high school kids push fries to one another's lips. We turn west on Calle Umarán and I identify the Berlin Bar by the people milling outside. Witt seems to enjoy a young rotational crowd that lets him recount new versions of old adventures.

Dean likes a crowd himself since he always gets attention, beatnik cowboy from another generation, tight body still catching girls' eyes. Inside, he seems to expect our table to be waiting and as if on cue two graying gringos rise from a primo spot followed by two young women poured into cocktail dresses, no doubt paid dates. Dean nods and one guy scowls when his escort smiles back. Dean's squint warns the dandy off and he pulls out a chair for me like I'm *his* date. We laugh and order a bottle of fine local tequila, Casa Dragones, my treat. Hernán, the *camarero* we've met before, smiles big. He brings limes in a silver bowl.

Dean licks salt from his hand, inhales his shot, bites lime, and grins. I sip mine the Mexican way, neat in a snifter, *sangrita* on the side. Dean's look quizzes my changed ways. From the corner comes Cole Porter's "I've Got You Under My Skin." The piano player croons, "I'd sacrifice anything ... for the sake of having you near." Dean's head bobs, fingers snap. I worry he'll hop the table to dance, but already he's scanning the room and I know what that means—as the tequila works to his groin he's forgotten our mission to find Witt. He'll replace death and dust with lace and lust, bear these memories into further adventure. Movement's so easy with no destination in mind.

Girls slink on barstools, huddle giggling in leather booths. One bevy of tawny beauties surrounds a weathered *gringo* in a dapper hat who's waving hundred peso notes at Hernán to signal *más*, another, *más*. Witt. Dean catches on even as he catches one of the girl's eyes. Never one to miss killing two birds with one stone, Dean sways across the room toward them.

It appears that Hernán acts as Witt's bodyguard and stops Dean mid-sway. When I arrive with our bottle Hernán tells us, "Loco in here tonight." Witt has won big in the *lotería*. And Mexican college girls come in droves here on breaks, looking for fun disguised as history. Then Hernán leads us forward. "I will vouch for you," he says. *"Buena suerte."* It seems that dealing with Witt demands luck, but we must have it. The small American smiles and bids us to sit.

The round-faced girl stands and Dean slides by her next to another, this one rubbing shoulders with Witt. No need for jealousy here, plenty to go around. I take the chair at table's edge and lean to ask him about Neal. The old man beams. One girl, Sara, moves to a chair beside me, close. Seems that at his age Witt offers more talk than romance. Yes, he knew Neal Cassady, drank with him back in the day. Nearly fifty years ago, isn't it now? Dean's got an arm around Gabriela now and barely pays attention to his potential guru.

But I do, listening for lies. The whole Kerouac crew here, Ginsberg spouting poetry on *La Parroquia's* steps, Burroughs bouncing a Mercedes along the cobblestones, all dancing with naked *señoritas* in *El Jardín*. Witt's full of such tales and the girl who's translating into Spanish can't keep up. Two other girls swing to the music, tired of old men's myths, it seems.

The piano man cools down with "Just One of Those Things" and I ask Sara if she knows the music. "Not Mexican," she says. "'Trip to the moon on gossamer wings'? *No entiendo*. What is 'gossamer'?"

Could be an opening, but I don't try to explain the delicate beauty of spider webs, instead ask if she likes "La Adelita." Raised eyebrows tell me she's doesn't recognize the Mexican classic either. "Pancho Villa's marching song," I remind her.

"Oh, *La Revolución*—a hundred years ago." Before her time. I've struck myself out.

Music and languages keep flowing. I dizzy and want air. I stand, hold onto the chair for support, and Dean hugs Gabriela tighter, frowns at me, the party-pooping disappointment. He's left me already. I apologize to Sara, leave Dean to his new friends. I slip Hernán a big tip and Witt reaches for our bottle, pours himself a long one.

Sunlight pours through the open balcony doors. Mornings are chilly in San Miguel and I wrap the sheet around me. Dean's stuff still clutters the floor like evidence of a disappearance. I make coffee, wonder when he'll come tottering in, all smiles or all woes, making me listen as he expands his myth. For the first time all week, I want to open the laptop's screen and tell my own version of how we romanticize our life, if someone else doesn't do it for us.

But noise in the street sweeps in with the breeze and of course it's Dean, keyless, calling to me. I look down from the balcony at him—more disheveled than normal, his short hair spiking, his face lined and pale. "Throw my stuff down, *mi amigo*. I got a train to catch."

There's never been a point in arguing with him, but I picture the non-existent train, the empty tracks. I can bait him with the chance to talk or just let him go. "Let's get breakfast, man," I suggest. "You can tell me all about her." But I imagine things did not go well.

Dean gives me his 'let it be' look, eyes sad above the grin. "Got to run, LJ. Something tells me my women miss me." If he failed with Gabriela, where did he spend the night? "Or come"—he catches my eyes, sweeps them along with his head to the south— "with me."

The sun glares over the hilltop mansions and catches me sheet-clad and shivering. I want to wrap him in next to me until I can warm him, slow him down if not hold him here. But Dean motions to hurry and I grab the backpack and bedroll, the trappings of his vagabond life.

His arms outstretch as if he'd catch me. I want to beg him to stay, stay *some*place, convince him by my example that to settle down is not necessarily to settle, that not to become a legend is not to be a failure. But there is no revising the tale Dean tells himself.

I make sure he sees me stuff some pesos into his backpack then toss it, light and musty. Dean slides the bag smoothly onto his shoulders and shouts, "*¡hasta luego*, John Little!"

He turns like a soldier and I almost call out, watching him march away, again unchanged. I imagine missing him when Teodoro plays "La Adelita" the melancholy way, when I revisit the station's hulking ghost, the wooden ties decaying into the sunken gravel bed.

He'll be alright, I console myself as Dean stumbles across the cobblestones, finds his tracks down the sidewalk, not once looking back and never one to leave a trail.

———◆———

(for SC and TH)

DESIREE

Susan Berkeley, tall and blond, drew notice walking along Calle Basilio Badillo's blocks-long stretch of shops, restaurants, and galleries. Strangers, both Mexican and gringo, followed her slim body more than her face, so here in Puerto Vallarta Susan passed as another well-off middle-aged gringa, perfect customer for the high-end merchants. She was glad to be anonymous on this new stage she had chosen. Only some beach reader familiar with one of her *nom de plume* Desiree's romances might recognize her from a book jacket's dreamy author's photo.

She scrutinized a mannequin adorned in a filmy white wrap that shimmered provocatively. It would better flatter her daughter Rebecca, but the girl, institutionalized in upstate New York, was near no beach on which to wear it. Susan's lapse into such regrets had brought her out tonight. She dismissed the shopkeeper's query with "only looking."

Susan maneuvered the street, surveying the fashionable goods in every window. At the Contempo Galería, a glass sculpture of red coral caught her eye. The colorful fan, eight-feet wide and five tall, would fill the foyer of her new condo with color. But closer inspection revealed cleverly twisted plastic tubing. Some things looked real only at a distance.

The deep tans of her new ex-pat acquaintances Charlotte and Jane, for instance. Both had wintered in PV for years and their skin—and poor Jane's frazzled hair—showed it. Wrinkled was not the right word, rather waffled or blistered, especially about the upper chest and arms. Of course, each had at least a dozen years beyond Susan's fifty. She hoped the sunshine here did not always demand payment in aging. She wished to disappear, not wither and die. Neither of these women knew her work, either as Susan Berkeley, author of two well-reviewed but poorly selling literary novels based on her childhood and escape from the Midwest, or as Desiree Ivory Skye, the pen name from which the past few years' romances flowed. She'd kept dreaming up the books' fantasy affairs at her agent Meg's insistence. Susan read Meg's increasingly desperate emails—what are you writing?—with a pleasure that balanced her dismay at receiving Rebecca's hallucinatory ravings. Susan rarely answered either.

Along the gallery's back wall, faux-Mayan ceramic heads topped display columns while vibrant abstracts surrounding them made her dizzy. "*Señora*, may I help you?" The clerk looked like Carlo, the handsome super of her East Village flat.

"Of course you may," she said, not attempting the Spanish she'd begun studying. "I need things for my condo at Los Raqueros." She hoped he knew the new beachfront high-rise. "Contemporary, Mexican flair. These paintings…is the artist well known here?"

"*Si, señora*. He has a studio in Centro. Or find him working on the streets, or beachcombing for ideas." He opened his palms toward a huge canvas of blues swirled with ambers, what might be boulders darkening surf. "He is in a museum in Guadalajara and has shown in Mexico City." He winked. "The city people, they love seascapes."

Susan had considered herself a city person, too, at least since she moved from Richmond, Indiana, to Chicago, and then to New York. She'd spent months in Southern California, too, "consulting" for the movie they'd made of one romance; a financial, if not artistic, success. She hadn't loved LA or its beaches teeming with youthful idyll. Here in PV's Zona Romántica things worked maturely, the moniker "Old Town" applying more logically than "city." She wanted to change everything about herself, let a new place in full sunshine compel her recreation. She'd picked Mexico's west coast since her New York friends visited only manic Cancún or Playa del Carmen on the east. They wouldn't imagine her reborn in the *mañana* vibe of the beach town.

"Well, I love seascapes, too, especially Mexican ones." She touched his arm in turning to another painting. "These are all wonderful, I think, don't you … *como se llama?*"

Perhaps the romances she'd written—and intended to write no longer—had driven her to the three affairs she'd permitted in her month here, one-time sexual confluences to purge her body with the comfort of strangers. Susan intended to pursue honest emotion in her new writing, figuring things out until feelings returned. Rebecca's collapse—likely permanent, they told her—would throw her into her own despair if she let it. The only positive outcome of her daughter's insanity, call it what it was—the proof of Susan's own resilience.

Her thoughts were sinking into the painting's waves when he replied, "I am Sebastiano, *señora, y usted?*" His smile seemed more sweet than hungry, boyish.

"I am Susan, and you can use '*tú*,' Sebastiano." She let his name roll from her tongue. "Strangers become friends quickly here, don't we?"

A week later Susan stood on her balcony overlooking Los Muertos beach. A group masquerading as Aztecs danced in feathered headdresses and body paint, playing drums and conch horns for clueless tourists. She'd bought the coral sculpture and two beach abstracts, expensive but settling the tone of her place; the sea's boldness brought indoors. Sebastiano proved anything but boyish both the night she bought the art and the next night when he hung it. Susan had broken her rules of "once only," even as she reckoned it should be Rebecca out sowing the wild oats of youth.

She strolled down Olas Altas, parallel to the beach. She hadn't seen Sebastiano since, nor answered his messages. Around the *zócolo* that centered Old Town, Friday night festivities swirled along with the dance troupe performing at the half-moon amphitheater. Susan stood among ex-pats and tourists thronged to *ballet folklórico,* Latin flavor in the Americanized environment. Twenty young dancers twirled in couples, a yard-wide ribbon stretched between each pair.

Susan wished Rebecca could see the show. Her only child had been an artist, talented at still life and portraiture. But three years ago, only weeks into her graduate school training in St. Louis, far from home, what had seemed random eccentricity became constant aberration. In frantic calls, she claimed spies were watching, her dorm room bugged. The voices she reported as bad dreams soon became waking commands—hide in the closet all day, dance naked in the dorm hallway, piss in the corner of the studio. Calls from the school—her antisocial behavior was getting worse. Had she done such things before? Never. No. Rebecca hadn't been the most outgoing teenager, but she'd attended plays, proms, concerts with friends of both genders. Susan searched memory for signs of problems deeper than the normal teen's. Nothing. Her descent came as unexpectedly as Susan's ability to switch writing gears from real life to romance.

She'd flown to comfort her haggard daughter, held her hand, asked gentle questions answered by silence or gibberish. Under observation, her daughter was diagnosed as schizophrenic, medicated, psychotherapied, and community counseled. But back in school—perhaps her peers stared or whispered—Rebecca had stabbed a classmate with a painter's spatula. Susan brought her back East and now, after a year of better and worse, in hospital and out, Rebecca seemed lost, still retreating into fantasy or blather. The upstate clinic failed to convince Susan her visits did any good, so instead she sent checks her romance novels would allow her to write for a lifetime. She promised to stay connected and Rebecca's emails arrived almost daily after Susan arrived in PV. Could her daughter believe—like a mother frantic over a missing child—that Susan had abandoned her forever?

The festive dance ended and graceful movement filled the stage. Susan watched a group of Mexican teenagers flirting across the street outside the elementary school, action so familiar she groaned. From behind the amphitheater, a tall, trim man emerged. Surely it was Jonathan Macklin, a fellow author—detective novels. Had Meg sent him after her? He glanced at the wooing kids and tripped on a slab of uneven pavement. He shook his well-tanned head and Susan realized it wasn't Jonathan, never tan in his life, a bookworm though wry fun at parties. The man smiled at his clumsiness and walked past her, down Calle Cárdenas.

Susan trailed after him, Jonathan or not. On the dark corner behind the school, she jostled his elbow, pardoning herself. She pulled up short and pretended she'd made a wrong turn. He asked if she was lost.

"Oh, not really." She balanced on tiptoes to better display her body. "Just wondering if Boutique La Rosa Rosa is on this street. Is a streetlight out?"

He walked her to the *tienda* that turned out to be closed, then to Lix for coconut ice cream. She didn't need to diet, he flirted. And shouldn't he walk her home? They discovered they were neighbors—perhaps why he seemed familiar. They slipped into her condo, lest they give their neighbors something to talk about.

The next day, the man dismissed before daybreak, Susan stretched on her balcony's chaise. Her sexuality had changed here. She'd never been promiscuous, didn't think herself so now. The sunny beaches, Latin men attentive to gringas, the well-heeled well-maintained older gringos, seemed like the magical strangers in her novels. She needn't answer to anyone—her publisher who profited too much to complain, her husband an ex for fifteen years. When Paul had visited Rebecca to offer Susan support, he'd showed sincere concern though he'd never wanted a child in the first place. Had she? After the tense meeting they shared tears. He made a pass and she gave herself over, but in the morning he'd left. Just as well. Their life as a family proved as much mirage as Rebecca's spies.

Susan scanned the bay south to the miles of hazy mountains framing the beaches at Las Animas, Quimixto, Yelapa. Was there a more inspiring spot on earth? But she spent no more than a minute at the laptop, not a single decent idea in her head. She'd intended to begin another novel with characters real enough to matter. Her literary writing once counted a few thousand serious readers. She moved to expensive New York, thankful Paul would continue Rebecca's support though Susan pulled the girl away with her into the unfamiliar. Then turned for money to the romance writing—one book only, she'd insisted—as literary approval proved less than enough. When Rebecca descended into illness, Susan recognized what a stranger her daughter had been to her. And while there was no better material for meaningful writing, the subject was too close. What authenticity could reach the page when Susan found her world unreal?

She let the sunlight melt her into sleep. When she awoke to the phone's ring, waves of dreams had washed away her worry. She wondered if it might be Sebastiano.

Instead her neighbor Charlotte reported that Jane had knocked on her door, concerned about "the stranger who visited Susan last night." She'd assured that Susan knew how to take care of herself, but at breakfast Jane questioned again. So Charlotte was making sure "you hadn't been raped by some *gringo loco*." Until the all clear sounded, there'd be "no rest for the wicked."

Susan imagined Charlotte winking. Over fruity drinks she'd confided that not so many years earlier a handsome young cabbie had "seduced" her and they'd gone at it in his backseat in a dark corner of the Costco parking lot. Now she told Susan any secret was safe with her, but do please be careful and remember that Jane—much more conventional—stood watch.

The horizon stretched over the Pacific, but no peace appeared even in the mix of blues with her anonymity threatened. She dismissed Charlotte's offer of dinner and conjured images of men from the past whom she'd desired but passed up, an artist immersed in her work. Anonymous now, anything seemed possible. Should she call Sebastiano, dare fate by turning fling into affair?

The afternoon wore on. Susan read, but her shoulders stiffened and legs cramped. She cursed Jane's intrusion and opened her computer, anger tempting her to write. An email from Rebecca had arrived. They sometimes came two or three a day, reports on what passed for her life, hopes for a future. Susan allowed herself two reassuring replies a week, not today. A long walk might help, but her mood demanded more, a massage at the spa next door, serious therapists safe from scandal. Other parlors were rumored to offer more fulsome relief. A man could find a "happy" massage provided by the gender of his preference. Could a woman? she'd asked Charlotte who returned a wink. Susan had gotten manicures here, and one massage a week ago when thoughts of Rebecca refused to stay north with the rest of her past.

The spa's waiting room shined—white chairs, tables, lamps. But in the massage room, dim lights made even the sheets shadowy.

Susan climbed onto the table and pressed into the face cradle, let the girl's hands find the sore spots Susan tried to describe, her Spanish failing. Her muscles popped and rolled. The masseuse, Maria, twenty-four, a year younger than Rebecca, ironed Susan's legs, forcing her to give up the tension. On the thighs Maria's thumbs dug deeper. Then fists gouged Susan's butt, pain so palpable she teared as the muscle released.

Warmth spread. Susan turned over, opened her eyes to see Maria smiling in success. Rebecca had glowed like that when reviewing a finished canvas. Maria gently worked her arms and hands, and Susan recognized music playing, a panpipe trilling over hushed drum. The girl's hands found the front of Susan's shoulders, pushed back the clavicles.

Susan crinkled her freed neck. The girl traced her jawline with two fingers, rubbed the small muscles around the ears, pressed free the temples. Then the fingers were gone, the girl whispered, "finished," and Susan sighed. She heard the door open and close, and cooler air breezed in. The room remained dark as she dressed, human connection ended.

Back in her condo, Susan showered, pulled the towel roughly across her body. She dressed in a loose shift and watched the sun set. Had Rebecca lost some battle of will with the calling voices? Her daughter had been methodical when painting, her extreme focus a quiet strength, or so Susan thought. The steep decline seemed an escape, but Rebecca made no accusations and the doctors assured Susan that such cases rarely exposed a clear cause. Rebecca's difficult delivery offered a clue—troubled pregnancies sometimes correlated. But though changes as she grew up might have been precipitous—Susan's divorce, the move between cities, especially Rebecca's distancing into an adulthood of her own—they'd never know. The sun splashed into the sea, burning the horizon with reds and pinks.

Susan went inside and opened her daughter's email. Rebecca sounded cogent, describing two sunny hours she'd been outside to paint. Her brush strokes were steady, eyes tuned to subtleties in evergreens dusted with snow. The wind that drove her indoors whispered Susan's name, then Desiree's, and Rebecca said she understood her mother was busy writing, that she needed her own outdoors in Mexico. Then she listed familiar medicines and doctors' names, reported the orders to stay calm that she heard from all voices, those both outside and within.

Susan rushed to finish dressing and resisted the urge to taunt Jane before going out alone. A block uphill she reached the Olas Altas hubbub. Salesmen worked the dinner hours, cajoling newcomers to tour condos or join barefoot cruises. She breezed past them and ignored the shouts that followed. Across the street she glimpsed a couple who looked like Margy and Ted O'Malley from Chicago, escaping the windy winter. She hadn't seen them in years, had barely kept in touch. Susan stepped into the street and a taxi honked and braked, its bumper a foot from her knee. She muttered apologies and rushed to the sidewalk café and her old friends' table.

"Imagine seeing you here." Susan smiled, trying to be as chipper as they'd remember her.

The man's eyes scanned up her body to her face. "Pardon?" The woman, at least ten years older than Margy would be, looked puzzled.

"Oh, I'm sorry. I mistook you for some friends from Chicago." She looked up the street for a landmark to ground herself.

"No, we're from Vancouver." The man had the funny Canadian accent she heard so often in PV. "Sorry." He returned to his plate and the woman nodded.

"Excuse me, please." Flustered, Susan stepped away but was jostled against a door by a group of gay men lost in their own chatter. Once the men passed, she checked her makeup. She must not let Rebecca's illness turn into her own guilt. Each of her romances—the novels—claimed guilt was the greatest enemy of all.

She looked back at the couple, nothing like the O'Malleys, really. What about sojourns in strange lands brought visions of familiarity? Homesickness, not hallucinations, thank God.

Susan realized she hadn't eaten more than fruit all day. She straightened and walked to Basilio Badillo, past restaurants touted to cruise ship tourists who scrambled in for overpriced fajitas and giant margaritas. She neared the gallery but to avoid it turned onto Calle Vallarta then up Carranza to a little Argentine place she visited regularly. She needed protein, steak, to cure her lightheadedness. Manuel, the owner behind the grill, welcomed her with a flourish of his chef's hat. His wife, the waitress Gardenia, seemed to have been waiting for her and delivered a mango margarita and spinach empanadas. She said these were complimentary for "*Señora Susan, nuestra amiga ... Señora Desiree.*" Gardenia placed a thick paperback beside the appetizer and Susan shocked at *Codiciar las Estrellas*, a Spanish language edition of Desiree's bestseller, *Covet the Stars.* The excited woman turned the book over and pointed at the photo, a glamorous version of Susan/Desiree. She was bound to be found out sooner or later. She put a finger to her lips. "*Es un secreto, por favor.*"

Gardenia gleamed. "*Sí, sí, señora.*" She asked for Susan's autograph, left the book, and moved to the next table where four well-groomed women watched the exchange. Susan arched an eyebrow, raised her glass and took a long sip until they returned to yakking. If they questioned her dining alone, who cared? If one of them put the Spanish, name, and book together and shouted recognition, her desire for anonymity demanded no more explanation than did Rebecca's illness. No matter how confusing, Susan would be herself.

She took a bite of the rich appetizer. Better to enjoy such flavor alone than to dilute it with prattle. One of the women—who looked like her college friend Patricia—nodded in Susan's direction as if to tell her, "been there myself." But of course the woman hadn't, had never savored exile, wouldn't survive it. Susan had gone beyond endurance to whatever this new place was—if not shelter, at least solitude.

She signed the paperback, "*Querida Gardenia, será nuestro secreto. Tu amiga,* Susan." Her steak arrived along with another margarita but Gardenia pointed to the signature. "*Inscriba* 'Desiree,' *por favor, señora.*" Susan sighed, signed, and knifed into the rare steak.

The table of women debated as they divided their check, preoccupied with propriety's minutiae. At least they had each other. Susan resisted the urge to pick up their bill, make life even easier for them. Had they left concerns at their northern homes, children who hadn't turned out perfectly, their promise unfulfilled? No, this lucky bunch would have passels of grandkids, husbands who golfed or sailed—or dead ones. Money in the bank to fret over. Susan chewed her steak greedily and when they looked back, waved goodbye like an old friend.

Susan declined dessert and walked up Basilio Badillo toward Insurgentes. Outside one of the massage parlors, three young women in tight white uniforms solicited men's business with smiles and broken English. What were they offering at this time of night? She gazed too long at one dark-haired beauty. "Massage for you, *señora?*" Susan reversed her path and hurried away.

Past Calle Constitución the crowd thickened for the Friday fiesta. A band played blues and rock to tempt the crowd to dance. Susan slid through the twisting bodies and rejected two older gentlemen's invitations to join in. The band began a frenetic take on "La Bamba." She stopped to take a breath. American music masquerading as Mexican, played by a Mexican band pretending to sound American. She questioned her own concealment. She had barely resisted Gardenia's recognition. Would she secretly have loved for the dining women to request autographs? She again felt herself between selves, somehow doubly alone. Without Rebecca.

Susan hastened on, window-shopping. The same mannequin wore the same white wrap and the same clerk came toward her balancing plastic glasses of wine to bribe customers. She took one, downed the bitter white. The alcohol sent sparks up her throat. Don't get drunk, she told herself. Was she drinking more in Mexico? She'd drunk plenty when Rebecca collapsed. At parties if asked about her daughter. With her ex-husband. The day after her ex-husband's seduction and days after her visits to the sanitarium. But never out of control.

The clerk offered another glass and Susan said "no," then accepted the wine. The Galería, and Sebastiano, waited three doors down. To kill time, she carried the dress and the wine into the dressing room. She stripped off her shift and noted that her tan lines had blended away. Her body aged well, but she felt dizzy. More drinking, yes, since Rebecca failed. And not even schlocky plots populated her imagination. Those familiar faces she kept imagining replaced memory and her hollow pleasure fought pain. Susan pulled on the sheer wrap. She asked the clerk to bag her shift. She would wear this new one.

Susan stood on the sidewalk. Her choices—head back to the band, now gushing a romantic ballad, or past Galería Contempo. In its wide front window her red coral had been replaced by a twisted bronze resembling a wave—or was it a horse? She felt as two-hearted as the sculpture, Susan or Desiree. But reflected in the glass she seemed transparent, anonymous.

Sebastiano gesticulated, deciphering the sculpture for a white-haired couple. The woman—she could be one of those Manhattan grandes-dames who gushed over Susan's books whether they'd read one or not—called to a younger woman who hurried over and shook her head 'no.' The husband gazed out the window while the mother gestured around the bronze as if defending its surreal shape. Sebastiano stepped near the older woman, a rapt audience.

Rebecca had appreciated Susan's taste in art, hadn't she? Two of her daughter's paintings graced the New York apartment, one in her study, the other prominent in the dining room. Susan had bragged about Rebecca at parties, though the girl shied away at compliments. Her daughter would hate this bronze sculpture, too—and the plastic coral.

Susan entered the bright space and Sebastiano excused himself from the family dispute. He walked toward her, hands outstretched. She allowed him to hug her, smelled his citrusy cologne, felt his breath flutter on her neck. "My favorite customer, Susan." He practically bowed to her. "Shopping again?" He swept an arm toward a wall of paintings.

She glanced around, but aside from the arguing gringas, she could pretend interest in nothing but Sebastiano. She considered leaving, enough rules broken, her heart not fully into another tryst. "No, I just came for the wine." She took a glass from a tray by the door. "*Y los empleados.*" Of course Sebastiano was the only employee in sight.

He laughed and stepped back. He hadn't phoned a message in days. "Why don't you look around, *mi amiga*? While I do business." He hurried to the family, solicitous smile returning.

Susan waited, sipping the tart wine and considering the paintings, a new batch of artists. One shouted "folk" with out-of-scale primitives of seraped peasants, burros, and washerwomen. A second offered the famous palapas and blue chairs of Los Muertos, tourists playing in the sun. In another, sadly familiar, a gringa lounged on her patio as a Latina girl served fruit and cocktail. Lives of ease among the hardworking but happy natives.

Sebastiano said something that drove the younger woman

muttering past Susan and out the door. Susan applauded her good taste in rejecting the sculpture but not her quick surrender. The mother laughed and gave Sebastiano a peck on the cheek. He laughed and gave a soft kiss back. The husband, wearing a resigned grin, pulled out his wallet. Sebastiano took the credit card and left them to further admire their bronze monstrosity.

As he processed the big sale, Susan angled beside him, shifted her hip to press his thigh. "You make a great impression," she whispered. "Come celebrate with me. *Una gran fiesta.*" She struggled out the Spanish, her flirtation a grand fraud.

Sebastiano kept watch on the printing receipt. "But I have business, *Señora* Susan. This street party and closing up." He stepped back, looked over her body, and sighed, too loudly to be sincere. "If I delivered a painting, perhaps. Did you see the new beach scenes? *Muy hermosos.*" He went back to the couple, receipt, card, and pen in hand.

Susan tightened her eyes, set down the wine, and left the gallery. She passed a hundred strangers, faces that recalled no names, not even false memories. Her legs wobbled and she hoped they would carry her to the condo, her fictitious home.

Susan had packed her luggage, emailed her realtor instructions to sell the condo. She warned agent Meg of her intention to return to writing fiction in which truth was not designed but discovered. She stood on the balcony, a shadow between condo's glow and moonlight reflected from the water. The waves, laden with sand and shells, swelled then emptied onto the shoreline with exhausted inevitability. As they retreated, they carried Desiree away.

Susan began a note to Rebecca and honest words appeared—failure, pain, fear, guilt. She capitalized LOVE and underlined a promise for them both. I will not leave you again.

She scrawled out a farewell to Charlotte and Jane. It would soon seem as if she'd never been there at all.

ONLY WITNESS

S TEVEN PULLED TO A SMOOTH STOP IN the left turn lane, on yellow. He tried to be careful when driving his mother in her car. During his returns to his forsaken hometown, her hands braced more and more often against the door at bumps and turns. At eleven in the morning, there wasn't much traffic, but from their left, a beat-up little car—a Cavalier—entered the intersection, a young man driving and a young woman in the passenger seat. Coming from their right a slate blue car, a large sedan like his mother's, bolted from its yield and swerved into the intersection. The white-haired driver's face pursed with confusion as her big car slammed the Cavalier's left rear, sending it forward into a wooden utility pole by the drainage ditch. Steven's mother gasped.

The Cavalier's front end crumpled, the crunch sounding even through their closed windows. The right rear door popped open and a bulky car seat slid out. A rounded bundle of yellow cloth skidded across the gravel berm into the ditch.

The old woman sat dazed, car now angled across the oncoming lanes. But from the Cavalier the young woman exploded, hands in the air, screaming, "Johnny!" Her unbloodied face contorted with pain. She saw the yellow bundle in the ditch, screamed again, and ran toward the blanket. Steven came to his senses. The bundle held her baby.

Steven began to back the car onto the shoulder, but his mother tensed and pleaded. "Oh, please, just get out of here." A siren wailed from a distance. "There'll be police," she said. She looked at him as if he were her only salvation. "Please, Steven. I can't take it."

She reached one shaking hand toward him. What could he tell the police? He couldn't have stopped the wreck, obviously the old woman's fault. The young couple was guiltless. No witnessing would make a difference. He signaled and pulled the car onto the road, then maneuvered between the old woman's car, a few people gathered, and the wrecked Cavalier. The scruffy young man sobbed as he pounded his fists on the car's twisted hood.

Steven eased onto the highway. He looked back to see the young woman on her knees as if praying—to the bundle, the stubbly corn field stretching beyond the ditch to a cold blue sky.

A State Police car sped by toward the crash, followed by an ambulance, then fire truck. Steven felt a guilty shock at not staying to report what little he'd seen. But his mother calmed and thanked him. She gazed out the window at the empty fields, nodding as if music played in her head. He'd watched similar nods at her kitchen window when water ran or teapot whistled, or bacon sizzled until its crisping roused her. Did the sound of the wheels soothe her?

Two months before, Doctor Held had diagnosed dementia or Alzheimer's, explaining that at this stage it made no meaningful difference. Tests wouldn't help, but maybe a psychotropic would calm her. His mother stared at colorful posters of body parts on the wall, at silver implements on the exam tray, the chrome arms of uncomfortable chairs. The doctor offered no further advice and Steven could construct no question. He could only manage her affairs, witness her decline.

Steven drove her through the fading downtown. Gaps between the brick buildings marked where a fire had decades ago erased a century of progress. The department store windows now featured discount electronics, records, and antiques. The drugstore where he and his father had eaten lunches at the counter was a "buy gold" jewelry shop. The Friendly Tavern was still the Friendly Tavern. The only vaguely impressive buildings were the two banks.

His mother, smiling now, pointed out sights, read out signs, paused in confusion when a gap grinned back with weeds. She hadn't driven at all lately, she said. Steven knew better. Her friend Lois had phoned to sternly recount a dinner where his mother removed her top denture to clear an irritant, rinsed with water, and reseated the plate without blinking. His mother had driven to Lois's house in the country, though how she navigated remained a mystery.

They pulled into the bank's lot and Steven caught her still staring out the car's window as if lost. Inside, his mother shakily signed the paperwork. The bank officer glanced at Steven as he signed new certificates he would hold there out of loyalty. Surely the manager had seen this situation before—the declining parent, the child assuming her financial protection. He owed his mother too much to steal from her, grateful for the funds she'd provided over the years. They had been essential in starting his art framing business in the city forty miles south. And she'd been generous with his ex, Lisa, so much so his wife irritatingly came to expect funding, money from his father's life insurance and sale of his accounting business. Plenty to see his mother through the two decades since his death and well into the future—more future than she had left to live.

The manager asked if she also wanted to close her safe deposit box. Had she brought the key? Steven needed help to identify the key on the ring she dug from her purse. On some keys she'd taped yellow notes: "garage," "back door," "office," though the last hadn't existed since his father died. Most simply dangled, useless as a child's charms. A teller led them, calling his mother by name, Evelyn, with kind gentility. Steven, alone with her in one of the vault's compartments, opened the box with hope to find the insurance, deeds, and whatever other papers he would need, sometime soon.

His mother sat, tapping her foot. He found life insurance in small amount, a title to the house and one for the cemetery plot next to his father's. He shuddered. He saw that the will was proforma, everything to him, his uncle Eddie the contingent beneficiary, longtime family lawyer the executor. Cash, $2000, suggested no doubt by Eddie, a right-winger who'd taken up the Apocalypse as his main cause. Steven's grandmother's thin wedding band was identified on the note which enwrapped it the fifteen years since her death. She'd chosen to stay in assisted living in her own small town 60 miles south. His mother had driven there every weekend for the five years Grandma had lived. He found her clipped obituary yellowing below one for his father.

Beneath the artifacts a photograph showed his parents celebrating their wedding, all smiles and hope. Another of baby Steven grasping a rattle in their embrace. He wondered if this morning's child might have survived the crash, if the parents possessed something else to hold on to. He should call the police, confirm the couple's guiltlessness; doubtful he would be arrested for initially failing to witness. But his mother sat, thin fingers tapping beats on the metallic table. His memories and fears pointed only one direction for her—to a nursing home. He needed to keep his mind on his duty.

Steven put the ring in his jacket pocket and gathered the papers. He handed his mother the photographs and watched her brighten. She pointed a crooked finger at the baby, puckering her mouth into a kiss. "That was you."

After the bank, she wanted lunch at Frisch's, a favorite of his childhood. She ordered a fish sandwich and he the Big Boy and chocolate shake. The female staff looked like they had three decades ago—chubby, hair-netted, unhurried. Once their waitress reckoned his mother's daze, she called her "honey" and gave Steven a tight-lipped smile. In the car, his mother complained his tip was too big and the waitress too heavy. "Fat people." She shook her head.

He wished she were so critical about the characters that morning who'd come by her house. First, two men in a pick-up offered "protective coating" for her driveway, the "asphalt" tank more likely holding thin useless oil. Steven shooed them away—Kentucky Travelers, they were called. A similar bunch had scammed his mother last fall—sticky black patches of dead grass at the drive's edges and the check she'd written for $800.

Then one of the Brummett boys—Howard, nineteen or twen-ty—knocked on the door instead of using the bell—did he know she was hard of hearing? Steven had left him raking the yard full of leaves, agreed on a pricey $15 an hour. The kid bothered him, but he wouldn't be hanging around town if he posed any real dan-ger. He tried not to judge.

Steven avoided the intersection of the accident—the investi-gation surely completed—taking a longer route past the Victorian houses along Albertson Street, their lattice trim decaying, roofs frayed, and windows patched with plastic and duct tape. Maybe one in five still charmed with the imperious beauty of persever-ance. But even that was cosmetic. The insides of the huge houses were probably ruined, or diminished into four-plex pathos. He'd kept track of real estate prices in the town's emaciated newspa-per online. Houses went for perhaps a third their value in India-napolis, his home. His subconscious was at work, he realized. His mother's house would have to be sold. He blanked out the guilt—it wouldn't change a thing.

The houses became shotguns and duplexes, then ranches of the '50s and '60s like his mother's own. He drove her subdivision's curvy streets and pulled into the asphalt driveway. The would-be pavers were nowhere to be seen. The Brummett boy had raked some leaves into piles around the front shrubbery and filled two bags that sat by the curb, but the job was unfinished, really barely begun. Why was he not surprised?

He helped his mother up the side steps then garaged the car with care—it was a tight fit with paint cans, flower pots, his fa-ther's fishing gear, and who-knew-what in boxes gathering dust there. When she moved out, the garage alone would take him a month of salvage, more months to clear the hoard of memories housebound. He remembered one brighter weekend he'd helped her at his grandmother's house. He'd teased his mother about a pack of love letters sent by her beaux. She must have had a dozen suitors—and they all sounded smitten, hearts aflutter in the romantic ways of yore.

Steven came inside. She was testing burners on the gas stove to place a teapot, one, two, three, until the right one lit, still wearing her jacket. Her face focused on the effort until she saw him and lightened. "Steven," she said. "You're finally here."

He helped her out of her coat and hung it in the front closet. The water boiled, she turned off the gas, poured slowly into the cup, mixed the instant coffee, and—yes—remembered the sugar. Such routine she could manage. As they sat at the table, he reminded her about the bank and their earlier errands. She nodded. "And the awful crash." Her body shook. "That poor girl lost her baby."

They spent an hour going through her checkbook and notes she'd scrawled near the phone. Doctors' appointments, donations sought, friends checking up—two with question marks by their names. Steven added in the deposited safebox cash and helped her pay bills. She strained with both subtraction and her handwriting, its elegance one of her prides. He double-checked her numbers as she waited as if for his verdict. The thought that she understood her own decline chilled his spine.

"No problems, Mom. You did great. Every number right." She smiled like a child. "You're fine, Mom. Plenty of money. You're still accumulating it, even the Social Security." He pointed at the checkbook. "You should spend more on yourself."

Her look scolded him. "Waste not, want not, Steven."

A knock at the door interrupted before she could question *his* spending habits. She sipped her coffee and he went to the door. Howard Brummett stood there with a smile forced on to replace the tough guy scowl he'd displayed that morning. "Hey, can you pay me, man?" he said.

Steven frowned. "Looks like you've got more work to do, Howard. Need extra bags?"

Howard surveyed the yard. "Oh, yeah, I'll come back tomorrow and finish up. I had some business." He rocked on his heels. "And I got a date tonight, ya know?" His fidgeting became more pronounced and Steven wondered if he was high.

"Really? How about I just finish this myself and you go enjoy yourself." Steven pulled two tens from his wallet. "What'd you work? Little over an hour?"

Howie huffed. "Man, I put in over two good hours. You owe me at least thirty."

Steven replaced one ten with a twenty. "Okay, but I think it'll be better if you find work elsewhere after this." He fixed on Howard's glare. "You understand?"

Brummett shook his head boldly. "I get it, man. No problem." He pocketed the cash and kicked a pile of leaves as he walked down the drive. "No respect for the working class. Sad shit."

While his mother napped, Steven filled four bags, but the trees held more. He surveyed the neighbors' pristine yards. At the Mains, three houses away, a bulky young woman swept her rake in broad strokes, pulling piles directly into a lawn bag opened by some metal device. She cleared a full bag's worth in three minutes, took a deep breath, and noticed Steven watching.

"Is that Stevie Scott?" she called out, her voice deep, red hair short and choppy as she waved her sock cap.

"MaryAnn Main!" He'd babysat her years before. All the Main kids were live wires, half-dozen different currents. MaryAnn, the youngest and only girl, had been a tomboy. He remembered how at four she'd kicked him so hard he screamed and had to cancel a tennis game with her brother Dan. He was glad the Mains—though reduced to father Glen and, it seemed, MaryAnn—were still there, familiar. Mother Pam had died a few years before, after a long and painful—but not mind-based—illness had strained the family. Still, the boys were lucky the daughter's sense of duty had allowed them to escape testing theirs.

MaryAnn walked over carrying the fancy rake, dropped it, and hugged Steven. "Evelyn told me you've been visiting." She stepped back. "But I hadn't seen you." She hugged him again, longer this time. "I wasn't sure if she ..."

"Yes, I'm really here." Steven looked her over. "And so are you—all grown up!"

They talked for a good fifteen minutes. MaryAnn did not live with her dad but did his yard work and cleaning. Her alcoholic brother Ben lived at home with father Glen, eighty and rocky in body but ornery as ever in temperament. Between the two of them more than a hand full. She checked on Evelyn as often as she could and found his mother's humor still hilarious. "Us girls can laugh about any man!"

She updated him on the other Main brothers—doctor in Chicago, computer geek in Atlanta, craft-beer hauler in Indianapolis, his friend Dan a carpet store owner in Louisville. MaryAnn lived with her girlfriend in a trailer park. They were poor but happy, she said, adding ironically that though butch, she was still the girl, thus responsible for her father's care.

Steven returned to raking and, as she joined in, mentioned Brummett.

"Stevie, he's bad news. 'Correctional facility' a year for cooking meth." She looked down the street. "Hangs around all over, doing odd jobs, mostly for old folks. Send him away." She tied a bag and lifted it proudly. "We watch him, Stevie. The town knows what's up." Was she suggesting he did not?

She refused his offer of a ten and promised to visit his mother more often and report. "When you're around," she offered, "we can have coffee and commiserate."

He woke his mother, told her about MaryAnn offering help, listed her grocery needs, and drove his own car there. Since Lois's call about the false teeth, he'd come once a week to make sure there was food in the house, that nothing had broken. A month before, the old refrigerator stopped running and she hadn't realized it until things began to smell, still awake at least to olfactory sensation. He'd thrown away the spoiled food, ordered a new appliance delivered, prayed she hadn't consumed anything fatal. Her appetite seemed healthy whenever he came. They went to the Big Boy or McDonald's, and he helped her cook, mostly microwave now, but also dishes she could reheat like meatloaf or mac and cheese.

He pushed the cart around the supermarket, probably buying too much. His running inventory of her diet guided him to replace what she'd eaten—Lean Cuisine Asian and Stouffer's pastas, frozen White Castle burgers, canned soups, crackers, bread and sandwich meat, cheese, and at least two kinds of ice cream. Chunky Monkey was her favorite and she always giggled, repeating the name. He bought Ben and Jerry's despite the price that would have driven her nuts if she still grasped relative costs.

Steven cleared the checkout, relieved he'd escaped familiar faces and small talk. But as he pushed the cart into the October chill, a high school friend he recognized approached, grin big as ever. "Steve Scott!" Paul Remington called out with enthusiasm beyond honest emotion. Steven hadn't seen Paul since college but had heard plenty. He'd been drunk driving in a car crash that killed his girlfriend. He tried to kill himself, disappeared for years. But here he was, surprised as Steven. "Man, what a trip seeing you. You can't be living in town?" Paul clasped Steven's forearm with demonstrative vigor.

Steven told him about his caretaking visits. Paul, now a landscaper, was up from Florida to spend a week on his parents' farm. His father still planted a few acres but this year would be the last—the soy beans sat waiting for Paul to harvest. His mother made ceramic pots, still sold some of them. He smiled with pride in her craft and asked if Steven's mother still sewed.

"No, she's pretty much passed that." What *did* she do all day? "Watches TV, reads. She worked until six months ago, kept books for Dillen's insurance. They finally insisted she retire." He wanted to know how Paul *really* felt, how he'd borne his guilt and come back from the dead.

"Man, don't I know. Scares me to think of my old man bouncing around on that tractor. I can barely hold her steady myself." He laughed, smile broad as a friendly dog's or a wolf's. "But I'm doing great. Here's my card. Tampa's a beautiful place." Paul gazed at the gray sky, still smiling. "A new life, man. A good one. Keepin' on keepin' on."

His mother didn't remember Paul, but as Steven stowed the groceries and carefully explained instructions for each package, he was glad Paul had survived his trauma and could pretend cheer. Any smile on his own face felt weighted with worry—his divorce from Lisa, an uneven business, a car crash with a dead baby. Far worse, his mother's decline.

He helped her mix meatloaf and reminded her how to bake a potato in the microwave. Her hands, crooked with arthritis, worked the ground meat, onion, and breadcrumbs. She hummed to show how much she enjoyed this act of purpose. Pride she still possessed. But neither that nor his care would save her from dying slowly, horribly. He was trapped along with her in a tunnel that, unless he managed to light it with denial like Paul, would witness only the passing darkness.

He tested her humor with the morning's paper's comics. Yes on *Peanuts* and *Family Circus*. No on *Garfield*. Her laughter at a weird *Far Side* clearly attempted to humor him. A friend had reported that his own mother performed stability for years, so she seemed fine to him while her failing was glaring to those who saw her often.

They ate and gossiped about her friends. His mother mixed up current acquaintances like Lois and Marie with those of the past—her maid of honor, her first job chum. Time scrambled inside her like a shaken globe, flakes of brightness falling in no pattern. Then she stopped talking and gazed at him as if she'd thought she'd been chatting with someone else.

He listened as she went through a nighttime routine of bathing and cold cream. She came out of the bathroom looking like his mother of long ago. They sat through an hour of sitcoms, she laughing occasionally and making sure he found things humorous, too.

She went to bed and Steven sat up another hour. A worn spot on the couch showed where she passed most time. Knitting needles and yarn on a side table. A coaster for a cup, a thimble, a deck of cards. He turned off the television and washed the few dishes. He checked the doors—locked, but the handles wobbled and he mentally logged another task for tomorrow. In his room, he moved the stuffed gorilla she'd saved, and filled his narrow bed of boyhood with no comfort.

In the morning he helped her find Pepto-Bismol in the hallway closet, placed a clean bath towel on the rack, loaded her laundry, suffered instant coffee as he read the Sunday paper from the city. His hometown's own paper, now a thin twice-weekly, would surely pass into memory soon. He watched his mother gather breakfast. Her test, he'd decided sometime in the night—if she can make breakfast, things can wait another week.

She put bread in the toaster, found the box of microwave bacon in the refrigerator and held it up for him to confirm, wrapped slices in paper towel and set the timer with a bit of difficulty, but left it unstarted. She lifted a grapefruit from the bin, halved it smoothly. In sequence she pushed the toaster handle, crossed to the microwave and hit start. She pulled two spoons and two knives from the silverware drawer and two napkins from the holder. These she arranged on placemats as the timer sounded and the toast popped. She set the warm toast on their plates, divided the bacon, placed plates on table, said, "forgot the butter," smiling as if she understood he waited for a mistake. "Go ahead with the fruit, Stevie."

She took a deep breath and found the butter and jelly on the refrigerator's cluttered door and placed them in front of him before she sat. Her movements seemed a waltz, his mother of old. He'd learned that Alzheimer's patients often did better in daylight than evening's darkening hours. She acted less nervous dividing the newspaper, then pored over the television listings in the entertainment section, pen in hand.

He skimmed the front section's news, and, while his mother found the comics, examined the first page of the Metro section. He hesitated before turning the page where waited news from nearby communities—crimes and car crashes. He read the notice of yesterday's accident carefully. John McIntosh, aged ten months, died in a crash on Indiana 9. His parents, Adam and Carly, were not injured. The driver of the other car, Margaret Smith, 84—older than his mother—was not charged, though the article suggested her blame. Steven remembered the McIntosh family vaguely. One of his generation, Jonathan, a few years ahead of him in school and rowdy, was perhaps Johnny's grandfather.

No further investigation, no point in Steven's testimony, nothing gained by letting his guilt linger. He swiped his eyes.

"What's wrong, Stevie?" She pointed to the full color *Snoopy*. "This will cheer you up."

Steven tightened the handle on the front door of the house, ran the vacuum, scoured the bathroom. His mother washed dishes and he dried as he'd done as a child on a stool beside her, learning responsibility. More leaves had fallen and he gathered them into a bag he set half-filled beside the garage. Maybe MaryAnn could finish the raking. And keep a closer eye.

Looking past the Main's house, Steven saw Howie Brummett on Clifton Street, trying to twirl a rusty rake like a baton that clanged on the sidewalk. Then he seemed to pretend to be a rock star with guitar, dancing clumsily out of Steven's sight. Headed where? To Louise Tripleton's or Barbara Kendrick's? A wealth of widows hereabouts, Steven realized, and Louise without children to watch out.

Inside, he wrote a note for his mother to show any potential workers: "All work on this property MUST be approved in advance by Steven Scott." He included his email, phone number, and address in the city. He wrote out several copies, and instructed his mother to give the note to anyone who came to the door asking for work.

"To help me?" She patted his hand. "I'll remember, Steven." She placed the notes under a fancy glass paperweight on a table near the front door.

Steven toted his bag to his car. His mother was slicing meatloaf for him. She would no doubt add some of the packaged brownies they'd baked. Used to be, she'd bake pie with scratch crust and fresh berries. Her desserts were as well appreciated as her sewing. Had been, he corrected himself.

Back in the kitchen the plastic-wrapped plate waited next to her key ring. "For you, Steven." She stood in a yellow-flowered apron she'd probably sewn in his childhood and pointed at the plate. "And will you pull the car out of the garage for me? I may have to go see Lois."

When he'd arrived yesterday, her car sat in the driveway. She must not have trusted herself to maneuver the tight-fit garage. "Mom, I don't think that's a good idea." He picked up the keys.

His mother placed her hand on the counter and straightened. She looked at notepaper taped around the wall telephone. Small sheets filled with scribbling recording her life.

Steven removed the car key from the heavy ring, the spare already in his pocket. "I've got to take this, Mom." She stared at him, the key. "You can call Lois for a ride."

She nodded, her face blank.

"I love you," he said, and put the ring of keys back on the counter.

She hugged him, but began to tear. "I love you, too, Stevie. Thank you." She wiped her eyes with a tissue. "For everything." She pushed the plate toward him.

Steven called MaryAnn. He'd leave the car key with her father; she'd drive his mother's car to the city the next weekend then ride back with him. He explained the plan to his mother, who repeated how much she liked MaryAnn. As they walked to the door, she asked about his ex-wife, but she'd forgotten Lisa's name. He wondered if she'd eventually forget his.

He pulled away from the house. His mother waved from the side door by the closed garage, her exaggerated smile showing her good cheer. He rounded the corner where the bags of leaves waited for pickup. More were falling from the trees. He scanned the house. There was more season-ending work to be done, from shrub-trimming to gutter cleaning. The roof's shingles were thinning, but the brick walls stood as solid as when his father built the house forty-five years before. Nothing more here to be done today.

He turned onto Clifton Street, then Albertson, then 15th Street leading to the highway where yesterday's wreck so disturbed his mother. Avoiding the intersection would call for ridiculous routes, postponing would demand a stop at the police station, possible arrest or not. But what comfort could he provide others, having found none himself? A word from a stranger would not ease the couple's pain, relieve what must be their feelings of guilt. Giving in to his own remorse would only deepen it. If there was any fault at all, it was the old woman's failing. He could not defend her, but he'd protected the world from his mother.

At the stoplight Steven entered the right lane to return to the city. Beside the tilted light pole in the shallow ditch, a wooden cross rose, painted white before the brown field. Beneath the cross a red-ribboned teddy bear and bundles of flowers waited for passersby to pile more gifts in memory of the tragic dead, to share the common grief of humanity.

Steven searched the car but found nothing to leave. He looked past the shrine across the open field. His grip tightened on the wheel as he made the sharp turn to drive back into town.

JIM POWELL founded the Writers' Center of Indianapolis (now the Indiana Writers Center) in 1979 as part of Free University. For twenty years, Powell directed the Center, building it into an organization that nurtured local writers and brought highly regarded visiting poets and novelists to the city. Powell's commitment to the Center, however, came at a cost: he stopped writing fiction. Following his involvement with the Writers Center, Powell taught composition and creative writing at IUPUI. Talking about fiction with his students—and a serious health scare in 2010—inspired Jim to return to his craft. Over the last nine years, he has written some seventy stories and placed a number of those in magazines. He holds an MFA in fiction writing from Bowling Green State University (1976) and in 2011 received a Creative Renewal Fellowship from the Arts Council of Indianapolis.